Left

of

Center

By
The Teen Writers Guild of
Piscataway High School

i

ISBN: 978-1-09-473848-2

This book is printed on acid free paper.

Cover Design Credits: Frank Sinatra
Back Cover Credits: Zachary Martin
Photo Copyright: Zachary Martin
Readers: A. Bandaris, Shelly Fredman, Frank Sinatra,
and multitudes who wish to remain nameless
Documentary: Frank Sinatra
Documentary videos and photos supplied by: Frank
Sinatra, Ronni Garrett, and Judith Kristen
Logo design: Frank Sinatra

Dedication:

To the Future Members of
The Teen Writers Guild of
Piscataway High School

Piscataway High School
Piscataway, New Jersey
Where the Magic began...

For those of you unacquainted with the City of Piscataway, New Jersey, please allow me the introduction.

Piscataway is located within Middlesex County, in the central part of The Garden State.

As for locale? It's a mere 35-mile drive from New York City, as well as within 250 miles of one-quarter of our nation's entire population!

And, within this unique gem of a city stands Piscataway High School, a gem in its own right.

The school, as well as the community, supports and prepares each and every student to become all they can be - not only as students, but as responsible, respected, and valued members of their local community and our ever-growing global society.

Our Writers Guild was formed to engage students in the joys of reading, to help them become proficient writers, critical thinkers, and effective, compassionate, and ethical communicators.

We do believe that you will see and feel all of that - in action - within each and every page of this book.

The City of Piscataway, Piscataway High School, and you, the reader, will be proud.

Founding Guild Members
2018/2019

Nicole Almengor

Kainat Azhar

Shannon Bertin

Ameerat Bisiolu

Siv Bjorge

Elijah Digirolamo

Yumna Enver

Ronni Garrett

Aisha Humaira

Anisha Jagdeep

Ankita Jagdeep

Anisa Kamara

Aliya Kazi

Semira Lewis

Zachary Martin

Oriana Nelson

Shreya Nilangekar

Rachel Oliva

Jordan Parchman

Valarie Samson

Dorothy Seaboldt

Zahraa Shaikh

Jenna Stickel

Claire Visscher

Barbara Wu

Karen Luo Ye

And, as it should be, the very first words from The Teen Writers Guild of Piscataway High School are ones of gratitude.

Personal Thanks from:

Nicole Almengor:

I have so many people I want to thank I don't know where to begin...

Thank you Mom, for always giving me that little extra push just when I needed it the most. Thank you to my loving friends and family for helping me move in the right direction so that I could live my best life. Thank you to Ms. Judith Kristen, who understood my poems and formed this lovely guild. Thank you to the Piscataway Board of Education for giving this wonderful opportunity. Last but not least, many thanks to: Kim, Allie, and Kirsten for listening to me, believing in me, and in taking on my case. Thank all of you for helping me to not only become the strong person I am today, but for also being my inspiration for all of my tomorrows.

Kainat Azhar:

First and foremost, I want to thank God, without whose will, I would never be able to accomplish anything I do. To my Mom, Saima Azhar, for without her love and support I may have given up a long time ago. You always pushed me to my fullest extent with kind and encouraging words. To my Dad, Azhar Chughtai, whose happy-go-lucky personality always makes me laugh when I'm stressed or feeling low. I appreciate how hard you work to make sure our family is not just satisfied, but happy, too. To my lovely, older sister, Rimsha, whose carefree and sarcastic nature is something I've always cherished. Thanks for supporting what I love and being happy for my happiness. To my advisor/friend/author Judith Kristen, who presented me with this amazing opportunity to work on this book. I appreciate all of the hard work you put into making my dream a reality. To our librarian Ms. Kathy Memoli, who is one of the sweetest ladies I have ever met. Thank you for being so determined to help anyone who walked into the library. I hope you always keep that smile on your face. To Piscataway High School, of which I am so proud to be a student, thank you for giving me the chance to put my voice out there. And, lastly, to my friends for being so supportive, thank you for providing me with the encouragement I needed. Your care and attention is what has made me happy and confident. Thank you all so much.

Shannon Bertin:

I would like to thank my parents, Saskia and Claude Bertin, for always believing in my abilities as a writer - more specifically - my Mom for buying me many books to entertain myself over the course of my lifetime. Thanks to my Dad - for spending every Friday night with me watching movies, which allowed my creativity to flourish. I would also like to thank my Tia (Aunt) for always encouraging me to read and write on my own - as well as reading multiple stories to me whenever she visited us. I want to thank all the English teachers throughout my life, specifically my freshmen English teacher, Mrs. Alonso and my 5th grade teacher, Mrs. Lau. They helped me improve as both a writer and a reader by creating a challenging yet innovative environment that gave me the incentive to push my abilities to their limits. Both Mrs. Alonso and Mrs. Lau truly believed that as long as I was doing my best, I would succeed. Without all of these people in my life, I don't think my love of writing or reading could ever be as strong as it is today. Last but not least, I would like to thank Piscataway High School for allowing the Writers Guild program to be a part of our school. This opportunity to share my work with the world is something I will never forget.

Ameerat Bisiolu:

There are so many people in my life who have led me to this point - all of whom I am most thankful for. First of all, I thank my family for encouraging my creativity – even when I said I didn't want to be a doctor. Thank you to all of my friends for being the perfect canvas for my characters and listening as I expressed my - sometimes crazy - ideas to you. I also want to thank Piscataway High School, not just for the creation of the guild, but also for being an exceptional place for me to fine-tune my talents. Writing is something I do to express what I believe are important topics that should be explored and emphasized. I am very happy and so very grateful that so many people are supporting me along my journey to success.

Siv Bjorge:

Thank you Dr. Frank Ranelli, Robert Coleman, Cathline Tanis, Piscataway High School, and a special thanks to Judith Kristen, for granting such an amazing opportunity.

I could not stand here with the inner strength I have today, nor the belief of my self-worth, if it were not for Kaplan. Thank you for teaching me kindness, patience, and that I do not have to live as a product of my environment. Thank you Brooks, for guiding me each step of the way, you have heard me even when I was speechless. You have encouraged me to keep fighting, even when I am not strong. Thank you Tara, for teaching me that, "tough times never last, but tough people do." Thank you for never giving up on me, and for all that you have devoted in efforts to show me that I do not have to suffer. Thank you Sam, for showing me that I am worthy of love, and being loved. I would also like to thank my teacher, Mrs. Villegas, for everything you have done for me. You taught me that kindness goes well beyond the classroom. And, along with Mrs. Viscardo, thank you for going above and beyond to invest in me, and taking the time to better me and my skills for a brighter future. Ms. Hughes, thank you for opening many doors in my life. And, last but certainly not least, I would like to thank my basketball coaches for the opportunities they have granted me. Thank you Coach Harris, and Coach Schneider for not only believing in me, but also teaching me to believe in myself. Thank you Coach Harris for acknowledging my strengths and helping me grow as a person. Coach Schneider, thank for everything you have made possible in my life. Thank you for teaching me that support goes beyond the court, and to stay positive, despite what gets thrown at me. These people have guided me through my darkest times, and have proven to me that there is good in this world. For this I am grateful, and I will forever emulate the kindness they have given to me. Thank you.

Elijah Digirolamo:
My deepest thanks goes out to all of my family. They gave me the love, motivation, and the inspiration to do so many great things! I especially thank my biological father, Scott Deats, who was the one who got me interested in superheroes and horror. I also want to most gratefully thank my amazing teachers: Mr. Longo, Mrs. Evans, Mrs. Blaszczyk, Mrs. Borrus, Mr. Stein, Mr. Watson, Mrs. Polishak, and Mrs. Margulies. I am equally thankful to my wonderful counselors: Mrs. Garcia, Mrs. Brown, Mrs. Mandell, and Mrs. Thein. Also, huge thanks to Piscataway High School for allowing the formation of this life-altering Teen Writers Guild. I thank Mrs. Judith Kristen for this opportunity! I heavily thank Francis Sinatra and Guild member, Ronni Garret for the production of the documentary for 'Left of Center'. I greatly appreciate Principal Lester, Mrs. Tanis, and Robert Coleman, Mrs. Memoli, and Dr. Frank Ranelli - without any of them, I would never have experienced this amazing opportunity with all of my fellow Guild members. Last but not least, I cannot forget the many magnificent writers who have gloriously inspired me: Stephen King, Edgar Allan Poe, and H.P. Lovecraft.

Yumna Enver:
I want to thank my family for shaping me into the person I am today. I also want to thank Ms. Kristen and Piscataway High School for giving me this wonderful opportunity, as well. Thank you.

Ronni Garrett:
My deepest thanks to my parents, Ronnie and Ronnie, for always encouraging me to do the best I can in anything I do, and, to never settle for anything less than I deserve. Thanks to my younger sister, Reanna, who forces me to be the best version of myself, knowing she eagerly and lovingly wants to follow in my footsteps. To my grandma for being my best friend and for always having my back. To my extended family for providing my life with such colorful characters. To my friends for giving me the freedom to be myself. To all of my 8th grade teachers who provided me with the perfect tools for the next chapter of my life, and giving me a school year I will never forget. To Mr.Stio for always being there to guide me in the right direction. To my high school teachers who have helped me grow and learn something new each and every day. To Rutgers Future Scholars for giving me a platform I never thought I would have in helping me achieve all of my creative dreams. And last but not least, many thanks to Judith Kristen for this surreal opportunity, and to Piscataway High School for allowing the creation of this most exciting, empowering, and personally fulfilling Writers Guild.

Aisha Humaira:
First and foremost I would like to thank my parents, Jaffar and Zeba Mohiuddin, for being my biggest fans and remaining confident in my abilities throughout the years, as their support is part of the reason I have continued writing as a hobby for so long. I would also like to thank my 11th grade AP English Language and Composition teacher, Mr. Storey, who fostered my passion for writing to an extent I never dreamed possible. I also want to thank the friends who have read my poetry and given me honest feedback throughout the years, as well as those who have inspired some of my best work. Last but not least, I want to thank Piscataway High School for giving me an opportunity to share my work and give it a platform I never thought it would have.

Anisha Jagdeep:
My greatest appreciation to my family, particularly my sister, Ankita, who helps me write and gather ideas for our poems and stories. I thank my teachers at Piscataway High School who have encouraged me and helped me improve my writing. I also appreciate the efforts of the members of the school board, Dr. Ranelli, Mr. Coleman, Ms. Tanis. Thank you also to

Judith Kristen for giving me the opportunity to contribute to the work of the PHS Teen Writers' Guild.

Ankita Jagdeep:

A special thanks to my family who gives me my greatest support and encouragement. I want to express my gratitude to Mrs. Doris Kearns Goodwin who captured my appreciation of President Lincoln and his literary and political work through her biographical book, *Team of Rivals: The Political Genius of Abraham Lincoln*, the best and most gratifying book I have ever read. I sincerely thank Judith Kristen for her efforts to create our book, *Left of Center*. I also thank the School Board, Dr. Frank Ranelli, Cathline Tanis, and Robert Coleman who helped bring about the Piscataway Teen Writers' Guild at our school.

Anisa Kamara:

First and foremost I would like to thank my mother, Inez Konjoh who has always inspired me to help others the way she has helped so many in need in Africa. Thank you, Mom, for always believing in me and helping me reach my full potential. I would also like to thank my sisters: Amira, Asiya, and Ernestacia, my aunts and uncles, my church, and my teachers for being an amazing team of personal cheerleaders. Thank you to my former English teacher, Mr. Hoek, who always challenged my creative abilities and saw the importance in my writing. Last but definitely not least, thank you to Piscataway Board of Education, Dr. Frank Ranelli, and Cathline Tanis – this book could not exist without you.

Aliya Kazi:

I want to thank my family, specifically my parents, Shahzad and Mozma, for always being there for me and encouraging my decisions. I want to also thank my brothers, Usman and Nabeel, for serving as inspiration to me sometimes, and for also cheering me on with my choices and offering valuable advice. I also want to thank my grandmother, Azra, for also being so kind and encouraging to me, despite our language barrier. And of course, Pearl for well… being the cute cat that she is. Along with my family, I would also like to thank my Creative Writing teacher, Mr.Longo, for his course, which honed my writing skills and furthered my drive to become a writer. I also want to show my gratitude to my English teachers, Mr. Hunt and Mr. Hoek, for helping me develop my writing skills and acknowledging my potential as a writer. And finally, thank you to Piscataway High School and Judith Kristen for giving me such an opportunity to share my work's passion.

Semira Lewis:

I want to thank my parents, Michael and Tadessech Lewis and my brother, Amari, for believing in me. I also want to thank my 6th and 7th grade teacher Mrs. Scotto for helping me make improvements in my writing. I want to thank my "siblings", Catherine & Elaisa, for encouraging me to join the writers guild. Thank you Piscataway High School for allowing such a great program to help promote aspiring artists.

Zach Martin:

My deepest thanks to my mother, Sueeney, for all the help and advice she has given me throughout my life. Thanks also to my brother, Trevor for being in some of my pictures. And, a very important thank you goes to my girlfriend, Rachel. I would also to thank all of the people who have encouraged me to do what I love. And last but not least, I thank Piscataway High School for the formation of the Teen Writers Guild.

Oriana Nelson:

I would like to thank my mother, Betty-Anne Nelson, for encouraging me to develop my writing skills. I would also like to thank my father, Curtis Nelson, and my Photography Club advisors: Alison Kuderka, Lexi Franchi, Tanasia Allen, and Mr. Lojko, for enhancing my knowledge of the world through photography. In addition, I want to thank my extended family and wonderful friends, to include Mrs. Harris, my seventh grade mathematics teacher who deserves praise as well. Without all of these magnificent people, I couldn't be as dedicated to my future as I am now. Many thanks also to Piscataway High School, Dr. Frank Ranelli, Cathline Tanis, Robert Coleman, Principal Lester, and Judith Kristen who made this Teen Writers' Guild possible. I am extremely grateful for this amazing opportunity that allowed me and my fellow classmates to share our art with the world. With all of our hearts, we hope this book inspires others to also follow their own beautiful dreams!

Shreya Nilangekar:

My deepest thanks go to all of my friends and family who read my work, loved it, and continually encouraged my creativity. Thanks also to my best friend, Mrunmayi, for believing in me, as well as my writing. Thank you to my younger sister, Shruti, for honestly providing me with a unique way to interpret life. Thanks to my first tutor, Ms. Elizabeth, who guided me on the path to writing, assuring me of all I was capable of creating. And last but not least, my deepest gratitude to my parents for encouraging me to live my dream. And, of course, thank you to Piscataway High School for giving me this wonderful opportunity to express myself to the world.

Rachel Olivia:

My most sincere thanks to my mother and sister, Christine and Rebecca, for always being honest in their praise of my work, as well as their ability to critique my writing in a respectul, straightforward manner. I would also like to thank my brother, Peter, all of my amazing friends, and my most constant fan and inspiration, Zach Martin. I also want to deeply thank Piscataway High School for allowing the formation of a Teen Writers Guild at our school, giving to us the ability to express our voices and experiences in many different creative ways.

Jordan Parchman:

First of all, I want to thank my parents, Jerry and LaVerne Parchman, for always supporting and inspiring me each and every day. Without all your love I don't know where I would be today. Next, I want to thank my entire family for always giving me their unconditional support in all my endeavors; your love has given me more strength than you could ever imagine. Next, I want to thank my dearest friend Ileen Acevedo for encouraging me to keep writing even when I felt uncertain or lost my self-confidence. It was your fiery passion and continuous persistence that pushed me to keep writing every day. Last, but certainly not least, I want to thank Piscataway High School, Principal Lester, Dr. Ranelli, Robert Coleman, Cathline Tanis, and Frank Sinatra for giving me this fantastic opportunity to be a part of something bigger than myself. The Teen Writers Guild is a chance for us young people to express ourselves freely in a way we usually aren't able to and I for that I could not be more thankful.

Valarie Samson:

Thank you to my parents for everything you've given me, especially your love, support, and encouragement to do what makes me happy. I certainly wouldn't have had the courage to join this writer's guild without you and my friends, who motivate me, and push me to try new things no matter how scared I am. To my dad, I love you so much and I hope you are resting well and finally free of pain. Also, thank you to my aunts, uncles, cousins, and grandparents, who supported my family and I through our darkest times, and for always being there for me when I need someone. Last, but certainly not least, a special thank you to Piscataway High School, Judith Kristen, and the Writers Guild for making this possible. I'm extremely excited to share my writing with others!

Dorothy Seaboldt:

I would like to thank my closest friends - Emily, Maritza, and Claire - for motivating me to write so many interesting stories, as well as inspiring multiple characters included in them. I would like to also thank my boyfriend Justin, for dealing with me throughout all of this and being supportive of me as I pursue my writing career. I would also like to give thanks to my mother, for starting my love of reading at a very young age, and continuing to re-enforce it as I got older. I would like to thank to my 8th grade English teacher, Mr. Lopez, who constantly reminded me that when I write anything, I have freedom! Last, but not least, I would like to thank Piscataway High School, and our principal Mr. Lester, Dr. Ranelli, Robert Coleman, Cathline Tanis, and Frank Sinatra, for realizing the importance of forming a writers guild and giving our high school students the ability to speak freely through art.

Zahraa Shaikh:
First of all, many thanks to my Mom and Dad for taking care for me and providing love and encouragement every step of the way throughout my life. I would also like to show my appreciation to my older sister for loving and caring for me. Thanks also to my little sister for supporting me, and to my little brother for cheering me on. I deeply thank my friends for seeing me through this entire project as well. Thanks to Shruti Patel for inspiring me to open my heart and write even more poems. I would like to express my gratitude to the staff of Piscataway High School for understanding how important it is for us to express ourselves and show who we really are through our chosen form of art. Last but not least, to Ms. Judith Kristen for all her help, kindness, and support to make this amazing Writers Guild the great project that it is.

Jenna Stickel:
I would like to thank my Mom - Carol, and my Dad - Barry, for always believing in my passion for photography. I would also like to thank some of my closest friends: Madi Zellmann, Kassandra Soma, Briana Rosa, and Brianna Labrada, who have been there for me throughout most of my sixteen years. I would also like to thank my amazingly talented photography teacher, Mrs.Lintini-Pombrio, for encouraging me to pursue my love of photography. Last, but certainly not least, my deepest thanks to Piscataway High School and to Judith Kristen who made this dream of mine a reality.

Claire Visscher:
I would like to thank my parents for their endless love and support. Thank you also to all of my friends for reading the things that I write and for giving me the feedback and encouragement I need. I am especially grateful for my best friend, Valarie Samson, who has always believed in me, been there for me, and encouraged me to do the things that I love

most. Last, but certainly not least, I want to thank Piscataway High School, Dr. Frank Ranelli, Cathline Tanis, Kathy Memoli, Robert Coleman, Principal Lester, and Judith Kristen for creating this amazing writers guild that made this book's collection of beautiful voices possible.

Barbara Wu:

First and foremost, I am grateful to God for every opportunity that I am given.

I would also like to thank my family and friends for supporting me and for motivating me in all of my creative pursuits. Thank you to my teachers for helping me develop my writing style and abilities, and thank you to every person who has inspired me throughout my life.

Last but not least, thank you to the authorities at Piscataway High School and Ms. Judith Kristen, who acknowledged that this guild would be an empowering, outside-the-box project for aspiring artists like me!

Karen Luo Ye:

My deepest thanks to my parents, Helen and Carlos, who have given me the slightest pushes I needed, and thanks to my siblings as well who give me the inspiration to keep drawing. Many thanks to the teachers who have taught me throughout the years, for expanding my knowledge and giving me so many chances and reasons to grow. Last but certainly not least, I want to thank Piscataway High School and Judith Kristen and all the people who were involved in making this book possible. It gave me this wonderful opportunity to share my work with the world.

The Lyrical Works
of
Barbara Wu

"Though no one can go back and make a brand-new start,
anyone can start from now and make a brand-new ending."

~Carl Bard

Real is the New Perfect

My songs are not perfect works of art
Sometimes they are hard to tell apart
It's difficult to make each one a star
When they all come from the same imperfect heart

My songs are not perfect storytellers
Sometimes they are hard to figure out
It's difficult to put the rhymes together
Without forgetting what the song's about

By now you must have realized that my songs fall short
in almost every way
But I love every song I write with all my heart
'cause that is where they came
So say what you want to say
But my songs are here to stay

My songs are not golden
but in my eyes they still shine
My songs are not daydreams
but in my mind they reside
My songs are not diamonds
but my heart they do reflect
My songs are not flawless...
but real is the new perfect

My songs don't have perfect instrumentals
Music theory doesn't come naturally
I still have yet to learn my fundamentals
But I am getting better gradually

My songs don't have perfect chord progressions
I still don't know exactly what they are
So I am fully open to suggestions
At least they might give me a place to start
By now you must have realized that my songs fall short
in almost every way

But I love every song I write with all my heart
'cause that is where they came
So say what you want to say
But my songs are here and here to stay

My songs are not golden
but in my eyes they still shine
My songs are not daydreams
but in my mind they reside
My songs are not diamonds
but my heart they do reflect
My songs are not flawless...
but real is the new perfect

I am not a perfect teenage girl
Sometimes I am too afraid to fly
It's difficult to master how to live in this world
All I can do is give it my best try

I am not a perfect human being
Believe me, I have failed more than enough
But I have learned that there's no gain in fleeing
Falling is a chance to get back up

By now you must have realized that your expectations
I could never meet
But I embrace with open arms my imperfections
'cause they make me complete
Perfect I could pretend to be
But I'm perfectly fine just being me

'Cause I may not be golden
but I shine in my own right
I may not be your daydream
but I don't need to fantasize
I may not be a diamond
but my heart I still reflect
I know I'm far from flawless...
but real is the new perfect

Flower in the Snow

This was the first song I ever started writing, and it was inspired by my experiences of growing up and inevitably learning about the darker side of the world. The message in this song is that even if everyone around you lives in shadows and becomes cold to compassion, you can still be beautiful. Don't let anything take away the beauty that is yourself.

A light in the dark
A flower in the snow
An innocent heart
A girl who doesn't know

She lights up the night with her radiant beauty
She brightens the sea with her tender white glow
She doesn't know darkness reigns in this cold-hearted world...
She's a flower in the snow

Ooh ooh ooh oh oh
A flower in the
Snow oh oh oh oh
A flower in the snow

A star in the sky
An angel from above
A beautiful lie
A heart that's made to love

She lights up the night with her radiant beauty
She brightens the sea with her tender white glow
She doesn't know darkness reigns in this cold-hearted world...
She's a flower in the snow

Ooh ooh ooh oh oh
A flower in the-
Snow oh oh oh oh

And if one day
A storm would arrive
Ready to make sure that nothing survives
Her strength will be tested
She may have to face what's in store
No hiding—anymore

And even though she may lose some of the shelter
That made life so happy and simple and free
Her roots will run deeper
She won't be so easily scourged
Not as fragile as before

She lights up the night with her radiant beauty
She brightens the sea with her tender white glow
And wisdom will help her stand tall in this cold-hearted world…
Still a flower in the snow

Ooh ooh ooh oh oh
A flower in the-
Snow oh oh oh oh
A flower in the snow

No More

I find that I am most creative when I am lying in bed at night, alone with my thoughts. One night, I felt that I needed to get away from my exhausted mind. I needed an escape, so I let my turmoil go in the most natural way I could: music. I began singing, softly, to myself. Somehow, what began as a lyrical mirror of my mind evolved into a painful story about love. This song is about pouring out your heart to someone who does not deserve it. Although the narrator tries desperately not to hold on to the shattered pieces of her relationship, her hopeless honesty at the song's end is a testament to the oppressive power of love. No matter how hard you try, the heart wants what it wants.

Your words
They mean nothing to me
Your promises
I know you don't intend to keep

It's all a game
You don't even mean what you say (anyway)
So why should I call you a friend?
You won't be there to hold me in the end

And I can't pretend that I'll stay with a man
Who can't tell me what's on his mind
But you still pretend that you'll never leave me behind

So how am I supposed to believe?
When all you ever do is deceive
If you won't give me honesty
How can I love you excessively?

Your charm
Ain't got nothing on me
The way you smile
Do you think I'm that easy to please?

It's all a show
You still act like you'll never let me go
But now I know
And I won't take it no more

How am I supposed to believe?
When all you ever do is deceive
If you won't give me honesty
How can I love you excessively?

I need to break free
And yet you still convince me
That you'll never leave
No, you'll always be right here with me

I need to decide
And yet you still deny
That you have something to hide

So how am I supposed to believe?
When all you ever do is deceive
If you don't give me honesty
How can I love you excessively?

'Cause I can't pretend that I'll stay with a man
Who can't tell me what's on his mind
But you still pretend that you'll never leave me behind

How am I supposed to believe?
When all you ever do is deceive
If you can't love me honestly
Why do I need you so desperately?

I need to break free

Kill 'em with Kindness

Despite its uplifting message, this song was created in a time of discouragement. I was frustrated by the lack of compassion in the people I had interacted with that day, and I felt pressured to compete with them. I felt that I had to be as outspoken, self-confident, and effortlessly cool as everyone else. Then out of nowhere, I came up with the first line of the song: "I don't care what anyone says". Yes, I admit, my haughty declaration was born out of spite, and maybe even envy. However, like most songs I write, the personality of the lyrics moved in a different direction. I was feeling anything but positive in that moment, but as I added on to my spontaneous creation, I found that my confusing emotions were providing the foundation for my very first "happy" song. If you asked me how my turmoil somehow wrote itself into an upbeat tune paired with inspiring lyrics, honestly, I would not be able to tell you. It's funny, how the heart chooses to express itself in certain situations. The heart is a mysterious artist, and it works in ways that are foreign——even to me.

I don't care what anyone says
All their silly little games
They won't get in my head
And I won't let anything stand in my way
I'll just kill 'em with kindness
Kill 'em with kindness…today

They might act like they're superstars
Always putting on a show
Letting everyone know
How confident they are
But it's alright
'Cause I'm doing it my own way
I'll just kill 'em with kindness
Kill 'em with kindness…today

There's no better time than now
Seize the moment, I promise somehow
You will find that joy is the best remedy for anger
Love is the best cure for hate

You might feel like you don't fit in
Like you're different from the rest
And you'll never be the best
If you don't know how to win
But forget it
You don't have to follow their way
So just kill 'em with kindness
Kill 'em with kindness...today

Stop competing
It's not a race
You might think you're far behind
But believe me, it's a lie
Why not go at your own pace?
And don't worry
'Cause you're winning in your own way
So just kill 'em with kindness
Kill 'em with kindness...today

There's no better time than now
Seize the moment, I promise somehow
You will find that joy is the best remedy for anger
Love is the best cure for hate

They will try to bring you down
They have done it before
If you fall, get off the ground
You don't have to take it anymore

There's no better time than now
Seize the moment, I promise somehow
You will find that joy is the best remedy for anger
Love is the best cure for hate

So don't rush
To get into this ongoing fight
Don't push
To show everyone who's wrong or right
There's no need to get carried away
Why not treat them with kindness…today.

Barbara Wu is a seventeen-year-old junior at Piscataway High School. She has always had a passion for literature and creative arts, but has only recently discovered her love for songwriting. After a year of privacy, she developed the confidence to share her original songs on her YouTube channel. Aside from writing, Barbara enjoys spending time with her family: Mom (Lan), Dad (Richard), two older sisters, (Nancy and Susan), her younger brother, (Joshua), and her adorable cat, (Kona). Some of her favorite hobbies are dancing, playing sports with friends, and learning about her Chinese heritage. After high school, Barbara hopes to attend Rutgers University. Her dream job is to write songs for Disney movies, but she would also love to become a teacher so that she can inspire the next generation of artists.

"Some people feel the rain. Others just get wet."

~Bob Dylan

The Written Works of Siv Bjorge

"It is not the strongest of the species that survive, nor the most intelligent, but the one most responsive to change."

~Charles Darwin

Mistaken Sensitivity

Shame on you. Shame on you for being so ignorant as to mistake *sensitivity* for *awareness*. As to look up at the sky and see nothing more than clouds. As to see a cemetery and think nothing more than tombstones. It aches in my soul for you to be so shallow as to mock the blind man for running into walls, and then have the *audacity* to question his limp; moreover, I cannot begin to conceptualize how you could dare tell that same man to stop feeling the air around him as he fears for the next wall to break him. It aches the same way as doth when you become disappointed at the sun for surrendering to the clouds. It aches the same way as you chastise the victim for the mess they have made... from *bleeding*. I must not refrain in the least, when I say that it aches in my heart precisely the very same way as to when you'd be so inhumane as to call me *sensitive*.

As if the sun is not gasping for breath as it struggles to shine light beneath miles and miles of lightning and thunder and rain, trying to prove its existence despite bruises from the hail, and the clouds in which smother its hope and drown its strength. And as if the headstones you tread over in the cemetery were not those of once living beings, who through tragedy succumbed to fate. Perhaps they loved, perhaps they lost, perhaps they lived. So tell me, has it ever dawned on your two-dimensional mind that just maybe there is more, *beyond* the surface? That every tree from a seed, in which is held bound by such roots? Every bay unto an ocean? Every breath unto an exhale? That beneath my perceptions lie experience? That every scar I have, was once a bleeding wound? Every one of my fears comes from a memory. And as you speak to me and I begin to cry, do not be so selfish as to believe it is to do with you; because more often than not, I cry because I begin to question what year it is...wondering if I have time travelled back into the past that I tried so hard to forget. More often than not, your words are the last screw undone on the steel box I built around my suffering in order to shut it away deep inside my chest where I do not *dare* to dwell.

So, yes, I begin to cry as you caused the walls to disassemble and the only thing I can do is weep whilst the suffering attacks my body like a fatal virus. And more often than not, I find myself questioning your existence; wondering, if I threw a match at your skin, would it melt because you are plastic? And if I caught you by surprise, would you have no hair wig to conceal the seams by your neck? the very same ones that hide your fangs, as you are a Werewolf in a mask... A werewolf quite familiar to the taste of my blood.

Awareness and sensitivity are not the same thing. You call me sensitive because I possess the intellect to synthesize the analysis of my past—not only to predict the future, but also to understand the present. You call me sensitive because I have been hurt. But that does not make me weak. It makes me aware; aware of what people like *you* are capable of. I am aware that knives cause wounds, which turn into scars. So when I see something sticking out of your pocket, I remember my scars, and fear not your words, but your *intentions*, because I have too many scars.

And how *dare* you act as though scars like mine fade. How dare you pretend as if the blind man can not fall. That the sun gave up, just because you cannot see it behind the clouds. Those graves, that is someone's mother. Someone's daughter. Someone's father, someone's son. So do not dismiss that by saying, "it's just a myth." Just because you can see grey clouds, that does not mean the sun gave up fighting through the darkness. Just because you punched me lightly, you do not know if I already had a bruise there or not. And just because you feel as though your words spoken to me were not that hurtful, you do not know what else has been said to me. There is so much more beyond the surface that your ignorant, two dimensional mind fails to perceive.

Above all, do not ever call me sensitive. Do not ever underestimate my awareness for all the suffering and bad in this world. Do not *ever* fail to take in to consideration all the wounds which I am still trying so desperately to heal, even if some are years old. Because every hurt and every loss has robbed a piece of me. Suffering has stolen so much of me that I am hollow, and all I can be is *aware*.

Consequently, my walls are bound to collapse more easily. Someone must not have hurt you yet—someone must not have hurt you yet because you are ignorant, you are not aware. Just because unlike me, your heart has not been shattered, it does not grant you the right to call the broken *sensitive*.

Because we are not. We are *Aware*.

The End of Me, or the End of You?

Have I lost you to the storm?
For have our roots gone askew?
I fear it is too late to rescue you

The wind has destroyed my once, house of wood
You have neglected every chance to protect your child with stone
Have you not countless opportunities more than I ever could?
Perhaps I am not the only reason why I have no home

Were the ominous black clouds not a telltale sign,
Imminent and dangerous;
Did you really not know my life was on the line?

Thunder roared and lightning cracked
The rain poured as suffering fathomed fact
Trees fell as my safety burned
As fabrication and denial were all you learned

And there I collapsed as the current washed me away
Marking the moment you joined the crowd clapping for the
opening act
Cementing oppression as if my death were a play
You watched me fall as the earth floor beneath me cracked

Perhaps you thought it was the end, that I was too weak to fight
Mother Nature's evil
But every river unto another
Every mountain there is a valley unto another hill
From forest fires come ashes
And then the birth of something beautiful

Something has to end, to start something new
Is this the end of me, or is this the end of you?

Chaos for Clarity

May the river flow, without the flood?

May the leaves fall, without the wind?

May life carry on, without loss of blood?

May fawns become bucks, without their mother's rescind?

How must the sun rise, without the set of dusk?

How will the forest grow, without the raging fire?

How may the earth rest, if the dark is merely brusque?

How can life evolve, if the circumstance not dire?

Where would the birds go, if there were no mice?

Where could the wildflowers be, if there were no weeds?

Where will the ocean flow, when we melt all the ice?

Where would the circle not stop, if only the gazelle succeeds?

Why do we know how to swim, when we're meant to breathe?

Is it the clarity or chaos that were destined to grieve?

Illusion

Does it fill you with despair, to think that everything is but an *illusion*? To think that everything is not what it seems? To think that what you desire, will only destroy you in the end? To think one thing looks one way, only to have it turn out another? To swear something was real, only to watch it fade like the embers of a dying fire; leaving you to question... *Did it ever really light up?*

Like the starving fish, who was so desperately trying to see the light, trying to swim to the surface of the ocean, trying to escape the cold, bitter darkness of the bottom of the sea. But as the fish finally got there, as the fish finally reached the surface of the sea, enshrouded in the sun's warm rays; illuded by the light, perhaps the fish truly believed it had reached serenity; But, it was in this very moment, a shark had come. *And no longer did the fish see the light.*

Or the toad, who laid eyes on the utmost beguiling butterfly. For the butterfly's iridescent indigos, in which were bolder than any lightning bolt, harmonious yellows, in which were more peaceful than any sunrise, and passionate vermillion wings, in which-convincingly enough-burned brighter than any western sunset, seduced the toad. And when the butterfly fell too short, the toad seemingly had reached its 'treasure,' that is, until the butterfly reached the toad's mouth. For what once seemed so enlightening, was now intoxicating... poisoning the toad. *And no longer did the toad see the light.*

And then there's the bird, so innocent in its intentions. Who would have known, after venturing out to fill the discontent in its empty stomach and its chicks - an act of kindness in and of itself - would end in such tragedy? The bird never made it back to the nest. *And no longer did the bird see the light.*

Or what about the fawn, who had spent its life hiding from danger in a dark forest. The towering trees, somber shade, always concealing the light. Just for once, the fawn aspired to see this light, that which shines beyond the forest. Frolicking out into the meadow in which caressed its fragile hooves, the fawn was finally free. But this was far from the truth. A wolf chased after the fawn, swallowing its hooves after swallowing its freedom. *And no longer did the fawn see the light.*

The cruel irony of it all, is how we are ridiculed by our own beliefs— beliefs that what is fathomable is tangible. And one thing we all can do is fathom the light, that is, before we attempt to attain it. For it is then, that the callous illusions may bereave us of all hope, of all possibility, of all belief in the light. Leaving us to see behind what has deceived us, and for that we will never trust again.

Thus, victims of illusions have conceived that beauty is poisonous. Love is predacious. Effusiveness is vulnerability. Trust is deception. Reality is false. The light is not real. You see, it's an illusion. You think it's real, it's what you desire, that it will fulfill you, but that is not true. It is not what it seems. Because the light eluded the fish to darkness, the butterfly's beauty was poisonous, and the bird's love alluded it to death. They didn't see it coming, for how could one predict the very moment they succumb to fate? Moreover, how do you determine what is an illusion and what is real? Because there are meadows, but there are wolves too. How was the toad supposed to see beyond the beauty? Should we let these illusions stop us and interfere with our lives? Because sharks aren't hungry everyday. Should we base our decisions on the shark's appetite? What about the butterfly's wings, because we don't know how they'll taste? If we live our lives in fear, as if everything is but an illusion, we will never come out of the darkness, or quiet our stomachs. This is no way to live. But if we take things by chance, we perceive them how they seem, we would constantly be risking our lives. Perhaps that is the illusion. The world is full of light and dark, meadows and wolves, danger and ease. It is merely impossible to know what is real and what is not.

Perhaps the illusion is not on us, yet *in* us.

Siv Bjorge, fifteen, recently transferred to Piscataway High School from New York. Siv has been writing for years, and finds the inspiration through the struggles she has endured; developing a way to transpire them into strength in order to obtain a deeper perspective in life. Siv likes to push herself to ensure she will always keep growing as an individual. Siv aspires to serve in the military, and pursue a career as a surgeon. The motivation in her endeavors derives from her passion to help others, serve the community, and devote herself to making the world a better place. Siv played for the Piscataway Girls Basketball Team, as well as Piscataway Track Girls Track Team. In addition, she swam for Croton-on-Hudson Girls Varsity Swim Team in seventh grade, and a USA Swimming team in Ossissing, New York. She is the co-president of Piscataway Key Club and volunteers at a hospice.

"Your pain is the breaking of the shell
that encloses your understanding."

~Kahlil Gibran

The Written Works
of
Anisha and Ankita Jagdeep

"Life is really simple, but we insist on making it complicated."

~Confucius

"No one can make you feel inferior without your consent."

~Eleanor Roosevelt

Quotes chosen by:
Anisha Jagdeep

NATURE'S COOKBOOK
(ANISHA JAGDEEP)

The speckled blue eggs crack open; the red-breasted fledglings
eagerly peek out the nest.
The delighted robin mother sweeps through the clouds
to find their morning feed
As the soft cerulean wings of the butterfly flutter
long without rest
To find a ripe papaya, its succulent orange flesh to drink
(Hold the seeds!)
The frogs jump up from the lily pads, reaching for a bite
While the coffee-colored bears try their luck
fishing in the falls up ahead.
They catch a pink salmon and try to hold on tight,
But it wriggles loose and leaves the bears crestfallen.
How about honey instead?
The soft rain pours down and garlands the leaves of the treetops.
The animals take shelter, but the monkeys stop to grab
a banana…or two
While the caterpillars quickly nibble on the leaf
and scurry away from the raindrops.
In our house, my mother and I take turns
stirringand tasting our stew.
We all gather around the table while our dog wags his tail
for a morsel to eat
And all of nature, after a hard day's work, tucks into supper.
¡Bon appétit!

~THE FOLLOWING~

The following two short stories are based on Sir Arthur Conan Doyle's creations.

As we have both become such big admirers of his tales with Holmes and Watson, we both felt the desire to see if we could come up with some deductions of our own. We sincerely give our gratitude to Sir Arthur Conan Doyle for writing such beautiful stories with wonderful characters and hope we have done him justice.

We also thank the Doyle estate and hope we have not strayed from the original in any way and that our attempts at storytelling pay a fitting tribute to Sir Doyle.

HOLME'S DEDUCTION
~ANISHA JAGDEEP~

"Ah Holmes!" I cried as I immediately shut the door to our apartment to prevent the flakes from littering the floor, "It has been snowing since morning. You would not find any gentleman walking around the streets without a tight scarf covering his nose!"

Holmes said nothing. I saw him pick up one of his beloved test tubes and pour a little of a peculiar purple, almost lavender colored, solution into a flask. It was of no use attempting to chat with him when he was engrossed in his daily experiments.

I understood it was futile to say another word until he had completed whatever he was studying, but I knew I did not have much time to wait for him. I paced impatiently in a circle around the room and then sat on the sofa, all the while clutching the parcel I had brought. Holmes had picked up another test tube, suggesting that he was still much occupied with his experiments. I sighed quite loudly, hoping he would hear my sighs and appreciate the fact that I was not at all willing to wait for hours on end for his mind to conclude its concentration on some household science.

The snow was cascading in quick flurries, and the sky was persistently darkening, causing me great worry. My nervous grunts and moans did not make an impression on Holmes who still had his back toward me; why, it appeared he had not even heard my entry into the room.

My eyes were transfixed on him, making sure of any sudden movement by my friend that would indicate some conclusion to his 'important' work. I was prepared to walk out when, as if suddenly coaxed by temptation, my eyes wandered to a glass holding golden-wrapped chocolates on the table. Discarding my impatience for a minute or two, I grabbed one and slowly unwrapped it; it was then that Holmes ceased his chemistry analysis and spoke.

"My dear Watson, you could have sent me a telegram instead of suffering silently and tolerating my impertinent discourteousness. I would have gladly come to the train station without your taking the effort to come here and arouse me."

I immediately dropped the golden wrapper I had carefully ripped and sat bewildered at this unexpected remark of his.

"You would have gladly come to the train station?"

"Why certainly old friend," exclaimed Holmes, "It would not have been much trouble to come and wait for your wife's train to arrive."

"Now Holmes," I placed the chocolate on the table and slowly stood up, "Now Holmes, you had your back toward me the entire time I was here. I was watching you the entire time, and your brain was already occupied! I am of course aware of your miraculous deductions, but…all right, let me have it. Who told you I was here to ask you to come along with me to the station to pick up my wife?"

He smiled his ever-mischievous smile and bade me to sit down. He too sat down on his chair across from me and lit a pipe.

"You are puzzled by my comment. Forgive my saying that there is every reason for you not to be so."

"Holmes, you could not have possibly reasoned anything without observing me the slightest! I know that you have read my thoughts before, but this time, you did not look up even once." I stubbornly argued, refusing to listen to any incredible analysis he may have done, even though I myself had been a witness to it countless times. "You have been told by someone. Let me see, I did talk about my wife returning to one of my patients today. He was…"

"Come now old fellow. No one has taken the time to tell me. I did have my back toward you, but my eyes and ears were ever observant. I knew at once that you were unusually irritated by my focus on my experiments."

"Yes, that I will agree with. I did sigh quite stridently."

"Well, those sighs showed me that you wanted me to pay attention to you, but they did not betray that you wanted to leave and me to come with you. You had not taken your coat or hat off upon entering, so of course that meant you wanted to tell me something and leave immediately. You could have told Mrs. Hudson to deliver a message to me if your intention was to tell me something, but you did neither. Therefore, I deduced that you had hoped I would come with you to wherever you were going."

I listened earnestly as if I was a young toddler listening to an exciting fairytale of some sort. Even though I was amazed (as usual), I realized that what Holmes had said before was true: there was no reason for me to be so mystified in the beginning.

"You thought I was so absorbed that I was not capable of observing you. How innocent of you Watson to forget that my eyes typically never fail me. I saw you looking at the sky and falling snow, revealing to me that you were afraid of being late. You would not have been thinking of being late to see a sick patient because you would not have waited for me all this time, for my presence would not have been useful. I then heard the soft creasing of paper when you tenderly held the parcel you brought. The parcel must therefore have been wrapped."

"Well, that does not divulge the fact that I was bringing it to my wife."

"Ah yes. Well, when you unbuttoned your coat, I spotted a pink carnation on the lapel of your suit. You must have been to the florist's, for nowhere else can you discover a flower or even see a patch of green for that matter in this miserable weather. That also led me to believe that it was highly likely that that parcel contained a pretty bouquet," he teasingly added, "Now unless I am wrong about your faithfulness of character, Watson, that bouquet in that lovely gift-wrapped box is definitely a gift for your wife."

"No, you most certainly are right," I was about to surrender to his wonderful genius once again until I remembered the train station. "You did however deduce that my wife was at the station. Was that sheer guesswork based on the fact that I was nervous about being late?"

"Not at all. Your wife could have been at home, and you could have been late for dinner, for instance. I am quite familiar with how women are if their husbands are late. No, I knew you were waiting for her train. She could not have been at home, otherwise, caring and loving as she is, she would not have let you out without your scarf, however late you were, lest you catch cold. You have forgotten to wear it even though you did notice that everyone else had worn theirs, tightly, and covering their noses."

I could not help smiling at the humor he infused in his relation of his scientific deduction. I recalled what I said when I first stepped into the room. How foolish I was thinking that Holmes's mind was dormant when I entered!

"Thus, I sensed that your wife was out of town. And furthermore, I saw the hansom outside, the one you took to come here. The hansom stood there even when you entered, so I deduced that you had told the driver to wait for a while. I am sure the driver would not have agreed to this request in this dreadful snow if you did not tell him that it was urgent. I was then sure that you were going to meet your wife, and if she was out of town, you would have been going to pick her up. That is when the entire situation became lucid and simple."

"I should have known better than to question your ability, Holmes. Yet, even after you made your reasoning so obvious, I still am quite astounded, I tell you I am."

"Now I tried all I can to relieve you of your astonishment, Watson, and I am sure that after this long but delightful conversation we have shared now would have upset the driver outside and increased the waiting charges."

I was still silently pondering the matter over that the thought of the hansom and the station escaped me. I said to him, "Well, it was perfectly gracious of you to sit there like an unflinching boulder and continue your work when you knew I was getting increasingly impatient!"

"Forgive me, Watson. But do realize that you have just been presented with yet another wonderful example of deduction you can add to your collection. And it is only your fault if I descended into such talk. If you had only told me that you had been living alone these past couple of days, there would have been no need for me to explain any of my deductions now, would there? Still, it was rather selfish of me to keep you waiting just to bask in that wonderful amazement you have whenever I sum up one of my deductions. I do not mind paying the waiting fees, but do not unnecessarily increase them. Come Watson, I'll get my coat. Let us not keep the man waiting any further."

"Oh, the driver can wait." I thoughtlessly remarked as I picked up the chocolate I had laid down and took a bite, "Who gifted you these chocolates, Holmes? They are simply divine!"

"Inspector Lestrade gifted them to me yesterday. It was his wedding anniversary…for heaven's sake Watson! The driver can wait, but will your wife wait?"

When he mentioned my wife, my mind awoke. "Good heavens! The wife!" I instantly grabbed all the chocolates from the glass and concealed them in my coat pockets.

"My dear Watson! What are you…"

"It will take more than flowers to appease my wife, Holmes. Now hurry!"

A HUMOROUS TIME
WITH HOLMES
~ANKITA JAGDEEP~

The reader might be stunned to discover that I am, occasionally, a sufferer of boredom. I assure the reader that my time spent with Holmes is most pleasurable and engaging and that I am entirely in his debt for the abundant adventures with which he has gifted me; however, I must confess that there were certain uneventful nights which left me restless. November the seventh was one such night.

Holmes had had no client in a few months, so he was drowning his moodiness in his violin. The bleak, gray sky and the cold, bitter rain did little to help my own mood. The bullet in my leg had become a bigger annoyance due to the added restlessness, so I simply laid back on the sofa, inspecting the morning newspaper for any small signs of excitement with which I could disturb my companion's mind, which in turn, would impress mine.

"You need not bother trying to amuse me, my dear fellow. I have already taken the trouble of scrutinizing the paper to the last letter." I was thoroughly taken aback by this sudden intrusion upon my thoughts.

"My dear Holmes! You never let down your guard even though you disguise it exceedingly well! How could you possibly know that that was my intention?"

Holmes gave me a playful smile. "Well Watson, there is a short way and a long way to which I succeeded in my deduction. The long way, I used to check my prediction. Which one would you prefer to hear?"

"Well, since I am quite weary, as you hinted before, tell me the long way."

"It is all very simple in itself. Do not think I have not noticed your reaction to our sedentary lifestyle. I remember you sat down at the dining table this morning with a passive expression. I was busy filling my pipe, but I still observed that you kept glancing over at me and at the desk and sighing. At first, I erroneously concluded that you were sadly reflecting on my consumption of the cocaine last night. However, then…"

I raised my eyes in surprise. "You took that infernal drug last night? I had only begun priding myself that I had at last coaxed you out of that temptation."

He seemed to be adept in the art of disregarding words of disapproval as he continued his statement. "However, then you got up, went toward the desk, and took out your personal inkwell. You betrayed a slight sense of resignation as you emptied out almost all the ink into a jar. I remembered that you had only filled it a few weeks before, right after you had finished writing about our escapade with 'The Noble Bachelor', as you fittingly titled it."

"Well, what of it?" I interjected. "I wanted to prevent the ink from drying up."

"Perhaps you do not recollect it fully. At that moment, there was a loud, hurried rapping on the main hall door and I saw you instinctively pour some of the ink back into your well. I sensed that you thought that the anxious knocker was a potential client of mine as that immediate reaction of yours told me that you were ready to start taking notes. When nobody showed up, unfortunately, you drained all the ink out again and stored your empty inkwell back in the drawer. I found out later from Mrs. Hudson that it was only Mr. Jones who lives downstairs. He had forgotten his keys."

"I remember now. I suppose that I appeared quite disheartened to you."

"More than that, I'm afraid! You then gazed in the direction of your folders where you keep those little narratives of my cases with a vacant expression in your eyes. It was clear that you were actually waiting to take up your pen once again. You then went into your bedroom without a word of good morning. When you just now took up the paper after you came out, not knowing that I had searched there right after you had left, I felt that you could only be hoping that there was a story in there somewhere that was worthy to bring to my attention." With an air of satisfaction - and I might add, of pride as well - Holmes leaned back on his chair and took up his violin.

"I must say that you are a genius when it comes to picking up small details. However, I feel that your conclusion as to my designs of finding a case for you now is just so dependent on me keeping the same emotion as I did ten hours ago, that it is somewhat based on luck."

"Well, as I mentioned before, this whole analysis was just a means of checking what I had already predicted. I must remark, my dear Watson, that although it was very flattering of you to feel that my cases are such an essential source of pleasure to you, I must confess that I just finished solving one."

It need not be explained why I was struck dumb by this new comment. I had no knowledge of this whatsoever. "What! Well, it was perfectly generous of you to leave me in the dark!"

"No need to get upset Watson. I was just teasing. It was only a trifle. It was not even an actual case. While you were sulking in your room, Mr. Jones came up here to ask me if by any chance, I knew where his keys were, as he had misplaced them. He is, as you are well aware, something of an absent-minded fellow who I should be glad not to make conversation with if it were not for his undeniably strong knowledge on acids, which has aided me in my chemical endeavors. I only had to ask him two questions to find out that his keys were near his shoe rack."

"You mean that you didn't even go into his room? How did you do it?"

"Well, I saw that his boots were crusted with a little dirt around the edges. They also seemed to have been agitated quite a bit as there were some very small, straight marks running around the sides. Probably too small for others but…"

"Yes, yes. But what was your first question?"

"I asked him when he last left his room. I suspected that the last time he even stepped out of his door was at least a few weeks ago as he is so involved in his solitary study to think of any other entertainment. He replied in the positive. His confirmation explained for itself that he had ignored the absence of his key for quite a while. It probably was not in a normal place like his desk drawer or pockets which he checks multiple times during the day due to him using them for his little knick-knacks for his investigations."

"That does seem logical, I'm sure. But isn't that last part rather obvious?" Although my remark was somewhat crude, my friend knew that my behavior was only such because I was deeply interested in his narrative.

"You are right, Watson, but every small reasoning has its place in the synthesis of the final answer. As it is, the second question might have changed based on his answer to the first."

"Well, what was it, man?"

"My, my Watson! You are building a rather futile climax! I simply asked him to raise his leg for me. When he did so, I saw that the sole and heel of his boot were comparatively cleaner and that the jagged lines were more visible. The lines also were in a unique pattern with the lines starting from two white, square-shaped points. It was not unreasonable to say that he used a key to scrape the dirt out of the crevices. He did not seem to remember when I asked him, but when I asked him to look near his shoe rack, he found it underneath his shoe horn, which incidentally, was also covered with some mud. I suppose Mr. Jones must have stuck his foot into a mire on that rare outing of his!" Holmes ended his story with a small chuckle as if he was talking to Mr. Jones once more. To me, it was a bit mocking as I had missed this little, but interesting, scene.

"Very clever Holmes! But you seemed to have miscalculated during your narration. You said you asked him only two questions. I counted no less than three, myself."

He was unruffled by my teasing and only shrugged in response. "By the way Holmes, what was that short way which you used to guess my intentions with the paper?"

His eyes shone mischievously. "Simple, my dear fellow. I easily realized that you were very desperate for an intriguing headline. After all, you were reading a two-day old paper."

I can imagine that the reader is having a laugh at my expense. However, the amusement is readily shared. After some silence, we both burst out in a fit of laughter. I playfully tossed the guilty paper to him. I can surely say now that those rare moments of boredom, which I complained about earlier, were very easily mended by my dear, humorous friend.

GOODNIGHT FROM NATURE
~ANKITA JAGDEEP~

As the sun crawls down under the earth to shed light
on the land below,
The moon wakes up the stars and gets ready to glow

The wind stays still to allow the trees to settle down
As to not arouse the tired birds who have put on their nightgowns

The clouds wave farewell, gather the waiting raindrops, and make
way for the moon
While the cow prepares for her jump and the dish calls for the
sleepy spoon

The rivers clasp the rocks to lessen their pace
So the little fish can rest their fins and find their sleeping place

While scanning the world for open eyes
The moon reveals a sweet surprise

He bids the Sandman to use his magic sand
To make sure all heads are tucked in all the land

Pretty soon, the soft hums of slumbering children flow
through the air
Some resting in cradles or caves and others on their rocking chairs

As soon as all the lights have gone, the moon shines his own
And with tender eyes and a loving smile,
he stays awake, but not alone

THE SUMMER IN WINTER
~ANISHA JAGDEEP~

Nestled in my hollow, the cracking bark I hear,

When one perfect snowflake starts the chill in the air.

My warmth, disturbed by cold wind; I shiver and fear.

Snow bites my fur; summer is gone and it did not care.

The soft grass of lime green loses its sun and shade;

The honey center of petals hides from snowy sprinkles.

Long and hard, I suffer to count acorns for my trade,

But the songs of the birds remain sweet like the stars' twinkles.

Feeding their young ones, smiles oblivious to icy stings,

Eggs of ice blue rest under warm feathers of brown.

Welcoming the ways of nature and what it brings,

As I stand amazed, watching each flake float down.

Even when the winter seems relentless and slow,

Just know, dear squirrels, your laughter will melt the snow.

~Narrated by a Squirrel

NATURE'S ART GALLERY
~ANKITA JAGDEEP~

With a stroke of her brush, she splashes a whirlwind of gray
And paints little white specs which blur out the light of day

Outside, a chilly wind sweeps through the air
And tiny powder tumbles down from the sky
to adorn the trees everywhere

After coating the land with a new, soft quilt,
the artist dips back into the blue,
Mixing it with the white for those crystal icicles
which have their own hue

As she adds finishing touches to her own handiwork,
the frost settles down,
The ground stiffens into ice and the leaves start to frown

One more ribbon of white streaks across her canvas
and she takes a step away
Putting down her brush for another day

As the weeks go by, the ice moistens itself and loosens its hold
And washes the Earth to release all the cold

Meanwhile, the painter herself has already begun
Dotting her landscape with red and bringing out the sun

The little birds and deer cheer as they see
Her pour streams of blue down the edges,
bringing out the clouds where the fog used to be

Through each of her paintings, a smile is brought
So she stores them all carefully in their own little spot

For there is a long line of them that runs far
from where eyes can see
They all make up her art gallery

Each painting offers a different magic to each day but what it is,
only she knows for sure
As she has those tender eyes and careful hands that could only
belong to Mother Nature

Anisha Jagdeep is a seventeen-year-old senior at Piscataway High School. She has always loved reading and writing poems and short stories. Anisha, along with her twin sister, Ankita, spends her spare time singing classical music, reading the *Sherlock Holmes* series or books about President Abraham Lincoln, and writing short poems and stories. She also enjoys the classic films that were released during the Golden Age of Hollywood and occasionally watches them along with her sister and mother who are both equally enthusiastic. Even though Anisha plans to pursue engineering in college, she hopes that her writing will continue to blossom throughout the years. One prominent goal of hers is to publish her stories and poems and become a great writer. Her favorite writer, from whom she finds abundant inspiration, is Sir Arthur Conan Doyle, the writer of the famous *Sherlock Holmes* series.

Ankita Jagdeep is a seventeen-year-old senior at Piscataway High School. She takes a keen interest in arts and history and is fond of listening to Indian, classical, and light music from the 1940s to the 1970s. She also thoroughly enjoys reading the works of Sir Arthur Conan Doyle and President Abraham Lincoln. While Ankita does find pleasure in writing poems and essays, she prefers to gather story ideas from Sir Doyle's Sherlock Holmes Canon and tries to come up with stories based on its titular character and his dearest friend Dr. Watson with her twin sister. Other interests include singing, drawing, and martial arts. She plans to keep moving forward with her literary pursuits with her sister, Anisha.

"Life is not a problem to be solved,
but a reality to be experienced."

~Soren Kierkegaard

"Character is like a tree and reputation like a shadow.
The shadow is what we think of it; the tree is the real thing."

~Abraham Lincoln

Quotes chosen by:
Ankita Jagdeep

The Written Works
of
Jordan Parchman

"All progress takes place outside the comfort zone."

~Michael John Bobak

I Am But A Fleeting Wind

I am but a fleeting wind.
I rush through yellowed leaves and dash through
tangled hair.
Yet as each day passes, a new one begins
I disappear, gone, never there.
From place to place,
I travel here, then travel farther.
Floating, in the space,
And the world never falters.

I am unlike the trees who lay their roots so deep.
What roots are there for me who is only
temporary?
Once I am gone, all signs of me deplete.
My home, not here in the cities, nor there on the
prairie.
For you see, winds remain in motion for all of
eternity.

Where, then, do I belong?
Where is a home for me?

Endless Spinning

Trapped.

I'm trapped. Alone. Suffocated by this world. Choked by the grime that floats in the air. Quiet.

Powerless. Unable to move from this sheltered place. Left only to stare out endlessly at what lies in front of me.

Oh, what lies in front of me.

The radiant beauty of it all. How could one even describe it? The sky, how it shines! It is matched by no other. Up in this clear sky are clouds that float, thin as ribbons, soaring above a jewel, far greater than any mineral. Beneath those wispy, white curls exists my dearest treasure. The little blades of grass that shoot from the ground to the dark pavement that rumbles with passing vehicles, from tiny, furry creatures that scurry along the wide trees to the smooth-skinned children that joyfully tumble through the soft green fields.

Yes, all of these, I cherish even above the finest of silks. Yet, unlike silk ribbons, I dare not touch this treasure of mine. When the urge to poke a droplet of rain or to feel the road beneath my feet overcomes me, I still myself and remain poised. Arm extended gracefully into the air, I remind myself, my treasure is too far from my reach. To reach for it at all, alone in the dark crevices of this hollow place, I would drown in the depths of my greatest enemy.

But never mind that!

With my gaze locked on the world in front of me, I push these worries to the back of my mind and see only the leaves dancing on the wind. Through glistening eyes, I watch as children press their plump fingers against the wall of glass between us, parents trailing close behind. As the hours tick by, they carry on in boisterous crowds, laughing as they pass, or in quiet pairs, hands intertwined. Every now and again, I've spotted a few who pause, right in front of me. In those fleeting moments, I put on my best face, hoping with my entire being that this person will be the one to see me.

Some, I have found, seem entranced with the sky, far too distracted to glance my way. Others seem enraptured by a small device in their hands. They keep their eyes turned down at its glowing surface, and away from me, who stands so expectantly. A few even stop and look through the glass that separates us, staring into my world… though never quite seeing me.

No matter! Certainty surges within this little body of mine. I'm sure that one day the eyes of my treasure will fall upon me and I will be free from the world I despise. Free from the enemy that taunts me so.

Until that day comes, I find myself memorizing the faces of those who pass by. I'll need to know the face of my savior, whenever they come, right?

Oh! Over there is one with bright eyes and thin grey hair, pulled back tightly into a bun. Perhaps she's like me and dances to sweet melodies in the night. Though I'm not sure her body would handle it well, she looks rather frail for a dancer. I'd love to see how she gets by, but, oh! there she goes …walking away.

But look, there's another! This one with grey eyes, blond hair and a thin shirt. He, like so many others who have wandered past these parts, is looking down in his hands.

Tappity-tappity-tap-tap-tap!

Look up for a moment, would you? Look at me, would you!

But he too disappears as soon as I've spotted him.

These people, they speed by with such haste, it's difficult to catch one for even a moment before they're off to something new.

Who has time to stop and look at me, anyhow?

But I'll catch what I can, count on the slim possibility that one might be captured by my little round eyes and stare for long enough to see me. I'll memorize the faces of today with hope that tomorrow, one of those faces will find me. Who knows who it could be? Perhaps that little child by the tree, or the young, curly-haired woman in the blue convertible, or the man with brown hair and deep-set dark eyes … staring straight at me.

What's this?

I realize only now how nerve-racking it is to be seen for the first time in a long time. And to be seen with a gaze that's so unwavering… Through the glass, his eyes remain locked, curiosity filling those black pupils. His eyebrows crease and suddenly, before I can even process the severity of this situation, he takes a step forward.

What's this?

Beside myself, I feel some warm emotion ease its way into my chest.

Could this really be? Did this man actually see me?

Elation bubbles within me and my stance grows proud, fantastical thoughts piling in my head all at once.

This is it…this is the day!

Standing in my finest arabesque, head high, and shoulders back, I find myself waiting for this man to push through the withered oak door, triggering the bells I've waited to hear for so long. In an instant, he would arrive, turn my key, and finally see me as I have seen all my treasure. The gears would tighten, slowly. The steel teeth of the contraption I know so well would pull back, preparing to create beautiful music.

And, when the eternity of key turning was finally over… I would dance.

The song of swans would fill the air, and in that, I would finally say my goodbyes to this world that I've known, goodbye to my greatest enemy.

Solitude couldn't reach me from beyond those oak doors. There was no place for him where I was going.

I was going to run to my treasure, to embrace it. I was going to walk among those who have walked. To play among those who have played. To speak with those who have spoken. To openly *love* my treasure.

And now, as I stare back at the man with his deep gaze focused on me, I see more than just another passer-by.

I see a man who is kind.

I see a man who is righteous.

I see a man who is… picking something out of his teeth?!

In one swift movement he removes some sticky green substance, flicks it to the ground, and then disappears just as suddenly as he'd appeared.

So, he didn't see me.

What a charming fantasy. One I indulged in with far too much eagerness and must now scold myself for. Reality has hit me. Imagine, me among my treasure. It's ridiculous, nothing more than a dream just out of the grasp of my plastered fingers.

I am not a part of this world, I have my own world.

My world of dust and grime behind thick glass.

With no company but my own solitude.

This is my place. This is my home.

So, I will remain, my joints stiff and my gears dusty, watching the people of this world pass me by. Keeping dreams and reality separate, I will remind myself that my reality is this store, this display case, with blankets of dust upon my shoulders.

But, when it suits me, I'll dare run the risk of allowing my dreams to dance in my head - leaping and bounding.

Perhaps in these dreams I will feel my key turn, gears tighten, teeth pulled back and music playing.

Perhaps in these dreams I will be free from this stale world where I stand still and alone.

Maybe then they will see me. Poised. Beautiful. Glittering like a treasure. And spinning, spinning, spinning, endlessly...

endlessly...

endlessly...

endlessly...

Jordan Parchman is a sixteen-year-old junior at Piscataway High School, and, an aspiring, African-American, writer. Jordan is the daughter of two retired Marine corps veterans, Jerry and LaVerne Parchman. Because of her parents' careers, Jordan grew up in an ever-changing military environment; Moving from Texas to New Jersey and all the way to Japan, where Jordan spent much of her time on the road, and even more time in unfamiliar territory. As her surroundings continued to fluctuate, Jordan relied on the support of her family, along with the rhythmic tap of her keyboard to keep her going from day to day. The wide range of people and places she has encountered throughout her sixteen years has shaped Jordan's perception of life as well as forming her into the writer she is today.

"Let us remember: One book, one pen, one child, and one teacher, can change the world."

~Malala Yousafzai

The Written Works
of
Rachel Oliva

"There is no greater agony than bearing
an untold story inside of you."

~Maya Angelou

In This Perfect Town

In this Perfect Town

I walk along the small road turned highway

My vibrant silk-laced bag bounced on the sweat of my back

I look around. My ears are unusually free of music.

I notice the expanding buildings and roads.

I relax as I connect with the town that grew up with me.

You pass by.

You creep by, a beady eyed Vulture, not knowing the life of your dead Victims.

You beep your horn.

You grow excited when I glance at you. You think it's an invitation.

"Hey baby... You want this?"

I sink into my heavy sweater and tug at the fabric over my chest.

I deflect your air kisses and pick up my pace.

The now unfamiliar sky swirls and boils around me.

I feel hot in the *worst* way.

It *sickens* me.

I run home.

I turn my head every other second to see if you slithered back.

I run past my favorite park.

I don't belong here.

I escape from you and reach my home.

Never to walk that road again.

Slow down...

Please.

I refuse to grow up fast enough for This Perfect Town.

Their Heart's Dance

Like a rising sun in a sleeping soul,

Love can emancipate and hold you captive.

Can turn the most masculine man passive,

Its lasting spell can twist ones perception,

Careful...

Its charm can lead to delusion

That beautiful mirage we are all starving for

Leaving each of its victims in a trance.

Forcing one to crave no less than their heart's dance.

Love's hot haze creates an illusion,

Though love tricks, we fall for confusion

Although we fall prey

Expect no less,

For a bright sun in a dull world blesses.

Rachel Oliva is a sixteen-year-old junior at Piscataway High School. She has harvested an interest in creative writing ever since she was ten. Rachel has always loved expressing her thoughts and opinions in unique ways. She lives with her mother, Christine, her sister, Rebecca, and three cats- Kitty, Crater, and Ollie. She enjoys listening to music, singing in choir, drilling in JROTC, and spending time with loved ones. Rachel is often inspired by her favorite authors as well as her fellow artists in the Teen Writers Guild. She aims to one day be a member of Congress and make the country she loves a better place.

"Love and compassion are necessities, not luxuries.
Without them humanity cannot survive."

~Dalai Lama

The Photographic Works
of
Zach Martin

"The only people for me are the mad ones, the ones who are
mad to live, mad to talk, mad to be saved, desirous of
everything at the same time, the ones who never yawn or say
a commonplace thing, but burn, burn, burn,
like fabulous yellow roman candles exploding
like spiders across the stars..."

~Jack Kerouac

"Confidence"

In this photo is a friend of mine who hates the way she looks in photos. So I asked her to stand there and I took this photo. I did all the editing I needed to do and this was the final product. This is one of my favorite photographs, not only is it aesthetically pleasing, but it also has a much deeper meaning hidden just underneath the surface. It shows that even when you think you don't deserve something or you feel ashamed or insecure about something, you can still obtain beautiful results that should put your feelings to rest.

"My Shoes"

Put yourself in someone else's shoes. Really, think about it. The life leading up to where they are now, the decisions they made, the love they lost, the people they found, their very inner thoughts and emotions, what they like to eat on a bad day. Think about it. This picture was taken in the underground subway of New York, under a sign that read 'no sleeping or eating on the stairs' and there laid a man, unknown, seemingly lifeless whether literally or metaphorically. Passengers and tourists and daily passersby made their way to their destination without a single glance at the man. I was even tempted to wake him up. Who was this man? Why was he here? What led him to where he was?

"Order 66"

As a fan of Geek culture, this is a tribute to one of the most iconic
and groundbreaking movies in history. Digitally created, the piece
incorporated some notable elements of the intergalactic story of
Star Wars. Admittedly, it was a challenge to finalize the piece as
most of my scribbles etched in corners of homework never make it
anywhere else. I created this to push my limits and see my
capabilities and how far I could go as an artist.

Zach Martin is a senior at Piscataway High School.

Zach takes pictures because he believes that a photograph can capture what we feel and convey that same feeling to others.

Zach comes from a small family: Zach, his mother, Sueeny and his little brother, Trevor.

In his spare time, he enjoys writing, creating art, and watching movies. In addition to that, he also loves listening to all kinds of music, and spending time with the people he cares about the most.

Zach hopes to someday be able to teach others how to express themselves through the magic of photography.

"In order to be irreplaceable one must always be
different."

~Coco Chanel

The Written Works
of
Ronni Garrett

"The things that make you strange
are the things that make you powerful."

~Ben Plat

Skipping Back

I was eleven-years-old when my dad first took me to the harbor.

The breeze brushed softly against my curls and the small particles of water splashed upward tickling my arms. I smiled as the tide smashed loudly against the dock before gently fizzling out into a foamy whiteness. While I knew the color was a murky brown, the sun glistened over the water, reflecting a dark blue. I glanced up at the serene look on my father's face and I knew he loved it, too.

My Dad grabbed a rock by his feet before gesturing for me to do the same.
"No, smoother," he chided.
I grabbed a new one. *Flat and smooth*, I approved, drawing circles on its sides with my finger.
"Perfect," my father grinned, before walking me toward the harbor's edge.
He stared out, letting the wind brush his stubble, "Make a wish, and if the rock skips, your wish will come true." The words were barely a whisper, as if he was reliving a memory.
But the wistful look vanished as quickly as it appeared and in seconds his rock was skipping gracefully toward the horizon. He turned to me with a smile.
With a new determination I looked out, tightly clutching the rock in my hand.

With a gasp of release, the rock flew from my fingers, twirling toward the awaiting sea. But I watched with a frown as my rock sunk, like well...like a rock.

With anger I turned toward my father, but I almost collapsed when I was faced with nothing but air.
I hugged my jacket tighter as the feeling of loneliness crashed over my body.
"I hate you," I whispered, tossing another rock harshly into the blue depths.
I sank to my knees, sobbing for a wish that would never come true.
I jumped when something hit my feet.
I looked up, tears glistening in my eyes.

The rock came back.

My Mother's China

I dropped my mother's china plate today.
It shattered into a million pieces.
My family was upstairs so they didn't hear it.

If I glued it back together, will anyone notice?
If I put it back in the cabinet with the other China, will anyone care?
If they noticed a crack, would they ask?

Or should I throw it in the garbage?
Would my mom replace it with something newer?
Would they shrug and move on just that quickly?

Or should I leave the plate?
Trust someone else to clean it up?
Make it someone else's problem?

In half a second, the shattered China disappears and I'm staring at a clean hardwood floor. I stare transfixed at the plate in the china cabinet.

Did the plate even fall?
Did the pieces shatter?
Did anyone else hear it?

Then I ask myself,
If no one hears something crash, did it even fall?
If no one is there to pick up the pieces, did it shatter in the first place?
If no one hears it, did it happen?

If no one hears you cry, how can anyone help?

The World is Calm

Sometimes I turn my phone off
Sometimes I power off the television
Sometimes I shut my computer down

Sometimes I silence my speaker

Sometimes I slide the curtains open
Sometimes I let the fire burn
Sometimes I open up the window
Sometimes I listen to the breeze

The breeze is a sweet tickle in my ear, a cold chill on my
neck that sends a shiver down my spine.
The fire sparks create a shadow on my toes, a shadow that
spreads warmth up my ankles.
The cold and heat battle until my blanket gets draped over
my shivering body - the heat wins.
The breeze whistles and the curtains dance, catching my
attention.
Leaves shuffle against the curb waiting for the perfect draft
of wind. When the wind blows strong, the leaves take off,
flying in all directions, soaring as far as the breeze can take
them. As the wind falls silent and the leaves sit still, a dog
runs by, ruffling the area, and the leaves take flight again.

A child's laughter quickly fills the air as she runs after the bouncing dog. Her mother's voice calls the pair inside and the world falls silent again.

A cup of hot chocolate finds its way into my hands and I stare mesmerized at the melting marshmallows as they swirl around the mug.
The world outside stays silent and the fire seems to dim as my eyes fall shut and my body turns off.

Sometimes the world is loud
Sometimes life is hard
Sometimes people are mean
Sometimes things seem crazy

But...

Sometimes I turn my phone off
Sometimes I power off the television
Sometimes I shut my computer down
Sometimes I silence my speaker

And the fire is warm
The leaves are resting
The breeze starts to sing
My body turns off
And the world is calm.

Ronni Garrett is a junior at Piscataway High School. Ever since Ronni was a little girl she has had a passion for writing.

Ronni comes from a small family: Mom and Dad- Ronnie and Ronnie, as well as her younger sister - Reanna, grandparents, Delores and Cary, and a beautiful extended family. Her youthful dreams started as early as age seven, one of which was hoping to become an Oscar winning movie director, the second was to become a best selling author! Ronni even knew she would call her book, "The Life of a 2nd Grader" complete with the visison of its title scripted beautifully across the top in bright blue crayon.

While she didn't know many words way back then - every day, ever since, she has expanded her vocabulary, reading every book within eyeshot.

In her spare time Ronni not only enjoys her family life and friends, but also her two darling dogs - Bella and Cherrie.

In addition, Ronni loves listening to show tunes, creating music, filming movie shorts, as well as her own version of art-noir.

She also loves spending time with her best friends: Kaylan and Jordan.

"Courage is the thing that no one can take away from you."

~Chris Colfer

The Written Works
Of
Aliya Kazi

"Fill your paper with the breathings of your heart."

~William Wordsworth

Ocean

"Do you ever wish to get away from here?"

"What do you mean?"

"I mean…"

I woke up before I could hear the answer. I could hear the soft beeping from the corner of my room. I looked over to see the monitor standing by my side, hearing its light beeping as it measured my heartbeat. I turn my eyes back to the ceiling, trying to recall my dream. I couldn't see anything, all I heard was a woman's soft voice. I tried to make sense of her question.

If she meant if I ever wanted to leave this hospital, then that's clearly a yes. I'm sick of wasting my life on this uncomfortable, white slate of a bed. I'm so tired of feeling the weak, crinkly material of this gown brush against my skin. I'm sick of this paper-thin blanket. I'm tired of the doctors and nurses intruding on me every minute to ask questions or prodding at my skin with their needles and machines. I'm sick of the cops coming in and questioning me. I'm sick of the pitiful stares from the adults that walk down the halls with flowers and teddy bears in their hands that are meant for other people. I'm just so tired of it all…

However, I don't think I could travel further than that. I wouldn't want to leave the city, state, or country. Definitely not. I don't even think that's possible. Eden is not possible. I stopped believing in utopia years and years ago. So even if I did leave this place, leave this city, state, or country, I wouldn't find happiness. I would feel euphoria just by walking out of the hospital but it'll take a matter of seconds before I'm unhappy again. I close my eyes, feeling eyelashes tickle my cheeks. I didn't even bother to look at the clock on the wall. All I needed to know was that it was sunrise as the otherwise white room was painted with orange and purple.

During Sunrise and after Sunset are my happiest moments since a huge chunk of the staff would leave and I would get my time of peace. I wouldn't need to worry about my name being called for a test, worry about a doctor coming in to poke more needles in my skin, or to hear people whispering, "He had so much to live for, why did he do it?" and "Fifteen, huh? What a damn shame."

Nonetheless, I put up with it.

Only a few more days... a few more...

My eyes closed again.

"Do you ever wish to get away from here?"

That same voice, that same question. I slowly opened my eyes as I was enveloped by darkness. I saw no one, but the voice echoed through the room. That is until I started to hear sound. The sound of waves as water slowly started to lap at my skin.

"Away from where?!" I practically screamed into the darkness, trying to make myself heard through the water.

I could feel it starting to fill up my mouth, nose, and lungs. The voice did not speak for a while as I'm forced to struggle through the thick layer of water lapping at my skin and pulling me in. After deafening silence, the voice spoke again.

"Don't you want to get away from this cruel world?"

I blinked. I couldn't tell if my face was wet by either water or tears. What..? Why is she asking me this? I felt a gust of cold air as a hand reached out to me.

I saw a torn sleeve of what once could've been a beautiful white blouse. Out of it extended a bony hand. I stared at it in horror as it reached out to me and started to caress my cheek, cold bones blending in with warm flesh.

"Why are you so afraid now? Didn't you try to end your own life? In this same ocean?" The voice asked and I wasn't sure how to react.

"Why... do you know this?!" I snapped at her, refusing to take her hand.

She didn't respond. Instead, I saw strands and strands of long black hair as the hand went closer to my direction. As her hands traveled down, I was expecting them to choke me, wrap themselves tightly around my neck until I gave way. But instead, her hands went to pull me into an embrace, pulling me into a cold, pitiful hug that I didn't ask for. I tried to back away but I was trapped in the swarm of dead fish, long black hair, and tightly wrapped in those bony hands.

"Didn't you want to live here with me? In order to escape reality?" She asked.

Her hair parted, showing a skeletal face with long black hair and a torn white dress that cloaked her body. I tried to scream back but my lungs were overtaken by water and I felt my vision fading--

"Hey, Oliver! Oliver! Are you okay?"

I looked out the window of the car as we drove by the hospital. The same hospital that I once used to spend my days. Even if it wasn't for a very long time, it still felt like forever to me. I looked back to see my best friend at the driver's seat. Light brown hair framing his cheek and trailing down his neck slightly. He was looking back at me as the traffic light had turned red. As I grabbed a hold of my surroundings, I heard light pop music from the car's stereo.

"You were zoning out so I was wondering if you were okay." He said to me. I nodded my head. "Yeah, I'm fine. I just zoned out for a moment." I said with a soft chuckle. I heard my other friend click her tongue as she leaned forward from the back seat.

"Typical. You really gotta stop doing that, you scared the shit out of the both of us!" She scolded. Even if she seemed harsh sometimes, I know she meant good from it. I laughed lightly.

"How so?" I asked.

"You started breathing hea--"

"GO!" I cut off my best friend as the light turned green and the driver behind us was ready to hit the horn.

As he continued driving, I looked out the window again. By the road was an ocean. It was surrounded by sand and rocks. The sight of the ocean filled me with nostalgia. I know just nearby it was the old neighborhood that I lived in from infancy to the beginning of high school.

"You used to live here, right?" My friend behind the wheel asked, a smile on his face.

I nodded. I heard my other friend chuckle from the backseat.

"Don't get all nostalgic on us, we came here for some pancakes to celebrate our graduation, remember?" She asked.

"Of course!" I said before focusing my eyes on my phone screen.

"You just need to make a right and you're almost there." I said and my friend obeyed.

It didn't take long as we sat down on the newly cleaned table of the diner. I heard my two friends begin to talk up a storm as the smells of different breakfast food clashed together at once. I heard wonderful sounds. I could hear the humorous stories from my friends and the people around us, their laughter, and their carefree jokes.

The waitress came with our order and I found myself looking down at the cup filled with hot tea. For a moment, I saw blue clashing with black but with a blink of an eye, it was back to its milky light brown color. Taking a sip, I tasted the sugar that washed away my salty memories.

Of course, that was three years ago. The ocean, the hospital, the dream of death. It's all behind me now. I grounded myself down once more.

The joyous sounds from the people around me and the sweet taste of the hot tea in my hands. All of this could've been thrown away if death really had taken me all those years ago. If I was foolish enough to melt like putty in that tight embrace, this all could've been taken away from me. If I truly did die at that moment, I wouldn't be feeling the peace that I'm feeling now.

But most importantly...

If I died three years ago...

I wouldn't be here...

I close my eyes and allowed myself to become one with humility.

So... To answer your question, Lady Death, I would say no. I don't wish to get away from here. Not now. Not ever. I'm content with the life I have and I'm more than happy to be alive in this imperfect yet kind world.

Protagonist

It was at the brink
of a lonely moment at 4 AM,
when I asked the ceiling,

"What is my purpose?"
"It's simple,
you are the protagonist of this story."
God answered.
But I just played the deny card
and covered my ears.

As I forced myself to sleep,
I dreamt of a story
A mundane and typical
slice of life
with a sad protagonist
standing on stage
while the audience
shouts at her to get off and quit.

Written and directed in the first person,
the story goes on.
The heroine drags her feet again,
that unfortunate heroine being me.
As I'm forced to live out another day.
Scenes fly me by as
I helplessly stand there,
praying for a plot twist
that will rid me of
this burdensome role.

No matter how much I yell,
"I'm a phony!
I'm a sad excuse of a protagonist!
I was better off as a side character!"
It still won't go through!

When will this world finally understand
that I was not destined to be the protagonist?
That I'm just a sad excuse for one?
With an empty heart,
I asked to the ceiling.
"What is my purpose?"
"You are the Protagonist."
God said.
So I turned around in my bed
and went to sleep,
exploiting the gift of ignorance.

If this were a game, movie, or show
I'm sure, everyone would avoid it.
The story sucks,
the protagonist is pathetic,
and that's the bitter truth.

Prayer, prayer,
I'll say a prayer
in hopes that it'll help me improve.
To become a better person.
Digging in my heart,
saying words of prayer,
I found a relic.
It was at this moment,
that I realized something.
There was no room to feel sorry for myself,
and that there is a reason why

I was picked as the protagonist,
out of anyone else in this world.

Written and directed in the first person,
the story goes on.
The heroine drags her feet again,
that unfortunate heroine being me.
As I'm forced to live out another day.
However, instead of crying on stage,
I wipe away my tears and proceed.

As *the* protagonist
of this shitty story,
I'll continue it to the end.
Cleansing my heart of sin,
I am no longer the same crybaby
as I was in chapter 1.
Even if the last chapter is so far away,
I can still feel my heart shedding skin
and my character developing in between the lines.

I must fight,
even in this mundane slice of life setting,
to be the ideal protagonist
that this world deserves!
I won't die out so easily
like the protagonists in Shakespearean stories!
I won't allow myself to be reduced
to a tragic victim.
Accustoming myself to the smell
of rotting tomatoes,
I'll be the fulfilling protagonist that this world needs!

Aliya Kazi is a seventeen-year-old Senior in Piscataway High school. She was born in Staten Island, New York but moved to Piscataway, New Jersey at age sixteen. Aliya lives with her parents, two older brothers, grandmother, and cat. She enjoys writing poetry, song lyrics, and short stories. Aliya also enjoys drawing, video games, baking, and listening to pop music. In the near future, she wants to pursue Teaching as a career. Specifically to teach English and Creative Writing.

"Unless you love someone, nothing else makes sense."

~e.e. Cummings

The Written Works
of
Anisa Kamara

"When you cease to dream you cease to live."

~Malcolm Forbes.

Again

Is it a sin, to love again?
To crave the roars of a Lion's den
To fall in love with just one kiss is to
Fall into a deep abyss
To hold you in my arms real tight
Is to fight a never ending fight
To breathe the same air you breathe
Is to intoxicate my lungs with the poison
you'll leave
To walk with you hand in hand
And not know exactly where we stand
Is to grip the sides of living death
And have the fate of old Macbeth
Yet nevertheless... I love you so
From looking in your eyes, that I know
My love, answer me-
Are you certain that it is a sin to love again

How Many More

They say we are "too young to understand"
But I understand
We understand
The pain, the tears, the cries
The 17 Parkland lives
Shouldn't be denied
They try to oppress us
Distress us
To silence our voices with their own
They say "we don't know how the government works"
But we do
We observe and absorb
We learn from school
And from "fake news"
Just how the government works
They say we need not worry
"We've got in under control"
Until the next bullet
Dances under innocent skin
They say we shouldn't be scared
"It won't happen to you"
But is that a sure thing?
Or are you just lying?

7,182

7,182 kids' heartbeats stopped
At the trigger of a gun
Since Sandy Hook in 2012
How many more?
How many more children, teachers
Movie goers, concert attendees
Have to innocently dwindle away?
They claim school is the safest place
But I do not feel safe anymore
Young or old, girl or boy
We all come together
With one heartbeat, one cause
We are the change
The world so desperately needs
We are the change
The world so desperately seeks
United we stand, divided we will continually fall
Until we achieve liberty and justice for all

Who **You** Are

I am not worth it
Don't tell me that
I'm a diamond and I matter
When I know that
I'm as broken as can be
No one can tell me that
Beauty lies inside of my body
The world will agree
Only I can change me
Because no matter the circumstances
I cannot be accepted for who I am
I will never believe that
I am capable of being loved
Because my ghost excessively whispers
Am I really worthless?

(Now read from bottom to top.)

Anisa Kamara is a senior at Piscataway High School. From a very young age, she has enjoyed creating art through words and writing. Anisa has a love for nature and adventures to places she has never been before. She also enjoys photography, watching films, and playing the guitar. Anisa comes from a family of five: her mother - Inez, and three sisters - Amira, Asiya, and Ernestacia. Her aspiration is to one day be an activist and help achieve equality for future generations. As well, Anisa enjoys sharing knowledge of the global issues that plague the world today and listening to David Bowie, The Ramones, Fifth Harmony, and Halsey.

"If you're going through hell, keep going."

~Winston Churchill

The Written Works
of
Claire Visscher

"Even the darkest night will end and the sun will rise."

~Victor Hugo

Unsatisfied

I was thirteen when I first met my worst enemy,
Disguised as a friend who wanted to help me,
And I fell captive to her promises.
Promises of perfection and beauty,
Of happiness and security,
A promise of control,
That soon took control of me.

She gave me an escape
From the pain I tried to suppress,
From all my anxieties and stress.
She gave me structure,
When everything else felt like such a mess.

I listened to her every word
As they played in my head on repeat,
Blind to the fact they were filled with deceit.
She said she was helping me,
That she was the only one I could trust,
That she would make me happy,
But, to her, I was never good enough.
She told me that I didn't deserve to eat,
Pointing out everything that was wrong with me,
Picking apart my body and personality.
She was only satisfied when I was hungry.

I followed her every instruction,
Unaware of her destruction,
As my weight plummeted,
And my energy declined.
Numbers consumed each thought in my mind.
Of my life, she had taken hold,
But I thought that I was fine.

She brought me to death's doorstep,
Disguised as the path to success,
As the gateway to happiness.
I took a step toward the door,

Then saw a flash of reality,
Of her deceptive personality,
Of the damage she had brought,
How she poisoned all my thoughts,
All the lies I had bought,
So I turned around,

And I fought.

All of her orders, I disobeyed,
Doing everything that she forbade,
Challenging everything that she told me,
Though it brought me so much anxiety.

She criticized everything that I did,
Telling me that I was being stupid,
That, without her, I was nothing,
And I'd never be able to be happy,
That I was ruining everything,
Making me feel so guilty.
I didn't think I'd ever be free
From the tight hold that she had on me,

But I knew I had to keep going.

Her grasp loosened slowly,
And her voice eventually faded.
She no longer has complete control over me,
But, my mind sometimes is still invaded
With her lies and false promises,
Her criticisms and orders.
Sometimes I'm able to fight back,
Or turn away and ignore her,
But sometimes she manages to take hold
And I listen to her and give in.
I don't know if she'll ever truly be gone,
But I do know this...

I will **never** let her win.

Grey Clouds

It's hard to remember the sun is still there
When it's hiding behind the clouds.
Deep down, I know that it exists,
But it doesn't feel like it.
I know that it will come back,
But I don't know when.
And, eventually, I begin to question
If it will even come back at all.

I get so used to the gray clouds,
That I forget that it's not normal
For the sun to be hidden
More often than it shines.
Sometimes I forget what it's like
To see the sunlight,
To feel its warmth on my skin,
To see blue skies,
Instead of only seeing dark clouds
That block out all light.

I'm tired of waiting
For the sun to come back.
I'm tired of trying to convince myself
That it still exists,
That, behind the clouds,
It's still shining,
When all I ever see
Is darkness.

Every storm comes to an end,
But so does every clear day,
As every glimpse of sun
Disappears behind the clouds,
And any hope that I had,
That maybe, this time, it will stay,

That maybe it will continue to shine,
Disappears along with it,
And I wonder if it was ever even there.

Every little streak of sun
Eventually gets blocked again,
And every gap in the clouds
Eventually floats away,
And I'm left once more
In the same darkness,
Wondering how I could believe
That the sun would stay,
When I know perfectly well
That it will always just leave,

And I'm left waiting,

Hoping,

Wondering if and when,
The sun will return
And start shining again.

Perfection

Perfection,
Nothing more than a perception,
An evil deception,
A reflection
Of our own insecurity.

What they see,
It's just a tiny piece of me.
It's not reality;
Just pretending to be happy
Because there is no key
To break free
From the chains of darkness.

They see success,
But they don't address
All the stress,
The pain I can't express,
The thoughts I possess.
They all just guess
That everything is great.

The self-hate,
This darkness I can't navigate,
The end I contemplate;
Maybe it's just fate.
But a fake smile, I create.
To them, it's no debate
That everything is great,
So why can't I be happy?

Maybe there's something wrong with me.
Content, I just can't be.
My head is my own worst enemy,
But "perfect" is all they see.
Maybe "perfection" comes with a fee;
Expectations I can't meet,
Pressure I can't beat,
Always afraid of making a mistake.

Every wrong choice I make,
Put on display.
My head, I can no longer take,
But happiness, I fake;
Make my mask more opaque,
Don't let them see me break.
I'm okay.
Right?

Happiness, I can't ignite.
Maybe I'm *not* alright,
But I don't have the insight
Or the might;
This darkness, I can't fight.
I'm just trying to find the light,
Just trying to escape the night.
Perfect?

...Not quite.

Claire Visscher is a sixteen-year-old sophomore at Piscataway High School. She lives with her mom and dad, Susan and Andy, her sister, Audrey, and her two cats, Pumpkin and Mittens. Claire is a huge animal lover and has been vegan since she was fourteen. Claire finds expression through writing, mostly poetry, and composing her own piano music. In addition, she loves cooking, baking, reading, listening to music, running, and photography. She also enjoys spending time with her friends and family. Claire hopes to someday become an author and open a vegan café, with her books for sale, of course.

"Too often we underestimate the power of a touch, a smile, a kind word, a listening ear, an honest compliment, or the smallest act of caring, all of which have the potential to turn a life around."

~Leo Buscaglia

Claire Visscher

The Written Works
of
Valarie Samson

"Fill your paper with the breathings of your heart."

~William Wordsworth

Last Breath

Struggling to breathe, his chest rose and fell in an uneven rhythm.

The oxygen tank released his last breath of air.

Tears fell from his eyes and his mouth hung open, as if it was awaiting another deep inhale from his body.

It never came.

"He'll respond if we give him water," reassured my mother, reaching for the half-filled cup.

"He's ...not moving." My voice shook with the anxiety that had been building up inside me over the last few days.

He's not moving. I reminded myself of what I had observed just a minute earlier.

His labored breathing had come to an end, yet the oxygen tank continued - pumping relentlessly, trying its best to keep him alive.

Please, don't leave us.

I grabbed his hand after I looked to my cousin for support. She had tears trailing down her cheeks, too.

Please be okay. Please!

My body ached and I longed for more time.

More time.

I wanted to scream. But my lips felt sealed shut.

I can't breathe.

Hyperventilation overtook my body.

The second I began to exhale, I felt an immediate need for another inhale.

I swallowed the lump in my throat, and squeezed his hand once again.

On the other side of the bed, my mother fell to her knees, sobbing, and wrapped her hands around his hands. "Please, Jo. Please be okay."

This can't be happening.

His nurse walked through the doorway.

She knew immediately what had transpired. "He passed. ...I'm sorry."

Her apologetic tone was shaky yet firm.

She reached out to hug my mother.

My cousin did the same to me.

"No. He has to be okay," I whispered in disbelief, tears overtaking my voice.

You have to be okay.

You have to be okay.

I hate cancer.

Our hearts were more than just broken - they were shattered.

Suddenly the room felt claustrophobic.

Long distance relatives wandered into the family room.

His hospital bed and oxygen tank comsuming most of the area.

The television was atill angled at him.

The South Korean Olympics faded into a small, barely noticeable noise.

"He *has* to be okay!" I shouted, convincing myself he had a pulse.

"I *feel* something! He *has* to be okay!"

I broke down as the realization hit.

The last words he spoke to me ran through my head. *Thank you for taking care of me, Sweetie.* I sobbed, squeezing his cold, frail hand.

...Goodbye, Dad. I love you.

Breathe

There is no silence in my mind.
No peace.
Just my thoughts;
Revoking my motivation,
My self confidence,
My happiness.
Suffocating me.
I need a break.
I need to know how it feels
To be anxiety-free,
And protected from my own mind.

But I can't be protected.
I can't escape myself.

My mind;
It keeps me silent.
It gives me days where I don't want to talk,
Days I just want to be alone,
Days where my only smiles are fake,
And my sadness can't be concealed.

There are rarely days that I feel okay.
Days that I start to think, "Maybe I'll be alright."
Days that I don't care who watches,
Who listens,
Or what they think.

Days that I feel like who I really am,
Instead of the person I pretend to be.

On these days,
A genuine smile reappears;
And my mind gets to explore:
Everything my thoughts deprive me of,
And the lack of pessimism by which I am blinded.

But those days feel unreachable,
Too valuable for me.
Too good for my overpowering mind.
I *hate* my thoughts.
I hate the negativity that I can't elude.
I just want to close my eyes and forget that it exists.

Maybe someday I'll really be happy,
And free of the self-hate.
Maybe I'll feel like my world has been brightened,
Instead of these thoughts invading my mind;
Instead of only hearing my cruel subconscious.
Someday, I'll finally be able to breathe.

Valarie Samson is a fifteen-year-old sophomore at Piscataway High School. She spends every second of her free time: reading, writing, listening to music, or creating it herself.

Valarie quickly found writing and music to be an unexpected creative outlet for her emotions, as the two hobbies were the easiest ways for her to express herself. Although she grew up surrounded by a large and loving extended family, Valarie's immediate family was always small. She lost her father, Roel - commonly known as Jo, to cancer in the second half of her freshman year in high school. Valarie now takes part in her school's chamber orchestra and swim team, and lives with her mother, Frances, and an adorable puppy named Daisy. She is strongly supported by her family, and of course her best friends: Claire Visscher, Tim O'Reilly, and Dustin Copeland. And, while she is unsure of her goals for the future, she hopes that writing about her life experiences and sharing her passion with others is one of them.

"Remember, happiness doesn't depend upon who you are or what you have, it depends solely upon what you think."

~Dale Carnegie

The Written Works
of
Shannon Bertin

"Don't wait for the perfect moment.
Take the moment and make it perfect."

~Aryn Kyle

Can they Understand?

They will never understand what their gun caused.

The grief.

The fear.

The pain.

They can only see their own gain.

Where their suffering has been put to ease, another has grown.

Grown like the lump in the throat of a mother who laid her child to rest.

Grown like the feeling of absence knowing that a close friend was lost in the mess.

The families, the friends, can never comprehend

How today was the day they lost the one they loved most.

Someone out there with a gun decided

It was time for others to suffer.

A someone who was *unfit* for a gun -

But still got one.

The ones who must suffer will never understand,

How this person, so clearly disturbed, was able to get their hands on a gun.

A gun that caused so much devastation.

A gun that made everything more unbearable.

By taking the joy and the love out of life

Sucking it into a black hole of desolation.

It is not the gun's fault though.

It's the person who wields it that's to blame

But even then, is it truly their fault?

How were they able to attain the gun?

Oh, that's right...

They walked straight into their local gun store and bought one.

Bought the gun that would be the end of lives,

The gun that would make people fear leaving their homes,

Or, sometimes even just being alive.

How did this person receive a gun so fast?

Maybe the laws will change at last?

Maybe.

Are you listening?

They hear but...

They don't listen.

In a world with so many ways to communicate,

You'd think it'd be easy

To speak.

To have your voice heard.

But, more than ever there's a disconnect.

We're not listening to each other.

One person says one thing.

One person says another.

By the end of the conversation neither knows what the other has said.

This isn't only prevalent in everyday life.

It's taken a form in politics as well.

One side wanting one thing.

The other side wanting another.

In the end.

Who suffers?

It's the people.

The people who depend on their government to do what's right. The people are always the ones who suffer.

The people who work tirelessly with little compensation.

Where's the compromise?

Why can't either side put their ego to rest

And truly listen to the other?

Communication helps us to learn, to grow, to feel...

Whether it be through words or signals or even just a smile,

Communication is key to understanding one another.

So...

What happens when no one is willing to communicate?

Does the world only get filled with hate?

Is that what it is?

Isn't it beautiful?

I always try to see things in a bright light.

From people, to moments in my life,

There has to be something good.

No one is born evil

And I hope that no one is completely evil.

Depending on one's perception

Any event can be seen as good or bad.

I like to put a smile on my face

And greet the world with open arms

But,

Sometimes it's hard because the world around me,

Feels like it's crashing down.

Sometimes I'd rather just

Cry.

Be upset.

And isolate myself from the world.

But, even when I do feel like that,

It's helpful to remember that

There is always a light somewhere

Even when it's hard to find, it's there.

It's in the little things.

Someone holding open a door for you.

Greeting you in the morning.

Asking about your day.

Even when it feels like it's you against the world.

It helps to take a step back

And see for yourself...

Just how beautiful the world can be.

Shannon Bertin is a seventeen-year-old junior at Piscataway High School.

Ever since she was very young, Shannon has been a fan of reading and writing, And she's enjoyed creating stories and sharing them with her family and friends.

Movies and music are also a huge inspiration for her and she enjoys watching films as well as listening to music during her free time. Poetry is another new writing style for Shannon and she enjoys designing her poems around current world events. When she's not focusing on anything involving literature, Shannon enjoys being active, and she prefers stamina and endurance building sports such as: swimming, biking, and track over all sports that involve a ball. Shannon is currently being the best she can be on the PHS swim team.

"The only difference between the master and the novice is
that the master has failed more times
than the novice has tried."

~Stephen McCranie

The Artistic Creations
of
Karen Luo Ye

"I hold a beast, and angel, and a madman within me."

~Dylan Thomas

Within A Dream

This drawing was inspired by a song called 夢また夢 which translates to A Dream Within a Dream and is by an artist called まふまふ (MafuMafu). This song is about a male character trying to reach out to the person he likes which is his dream, but he doesn't know how, which makes him dream within a dream. The song was very catchy and while listening to the song I got inspired to draw the characters in the music video because they were very cute and I felt very happy while listening to it. I wanted to convey the characters as lost within their dreams with the monsters in the back cheering for them.

Treasures & Memories

This piece was inspired by the things that I own and I like. I decided to draw all of them in one place. All the items in the drawing above are things that I am interested in, or have in my possession, or symbols of shows that I really liked, and they give a nostalgic feeling whenever I look at them. I wanted to see all the things that I love on one paper because it is a piece that kind of shows a lot about the things that intrigue me.

Lucky To Have

The person is from the band, BTS, whose music I have been listening to recently. Music and art in general have inspired me throughout many years of my life and I hold them both close to my heart. Since I use them to cope and escape from time to time, they are some of the most important things that I treasure.

Built Up

This piece was inspired by the poem "Amnesia", written by Aisha Humaira. After reading the poem I gained the image of a sad, broken person. But after reading it again, with some added insight on the background from the poem's author, I gained a new image. This shows a person who has gotten sick of all the things that were thrown at her and now has an attitude of "You can't hurt me" that is displayed through her expression and the wings around her are protecting her from the situations that used to be so hurtful.

Karen Luo Ye is a sophomore at Piscataway High School and has always enjoyed drawing during her free time and during class.

She lives 365 days a year in which she spends 180 of them attending school. You can find her subtly paying attention during class while doodling in her notebook during those 180 days. She has always been drawing and always admired the illustrations that were in all the books that she has read.

She resides in a house with her somewhat large family of six that consists of her mom, Helen, and her dad, Carlos and her two brothers, Michel and Bryan and her twin sister, Pauline. In her spare time you can catch her drawing (of course), reading, listening to her favorite music, watching TV shows and anime or doing paper crafts.

"My mission in life is not merely to survive, but to thrive; and to do so with some passion, some compassion, some humor, and some style."

~Maya Angelou

The Written Works
of
Nicole Almengor

"The two most important days in your life
are the day you are born and the day you find out why."

~Mark Twain

No longer a Princess

She was a princess.
She had a dazzling smile and she was always happy,
She was kind to everyone and she was everyone's sun.

Then one day it just stopped,
It stopped because of him.

A monster is what he was.

Every touch felt like fire against her skin –
Every time she begged him to stop, he would tell her to shut up –
She felt like she was being torn up from the inside out,
Kicking and screaming and then –

She just stopped.

She no longer felt like a princess,
She felt like she was no longer there,

like she was dead,
and didn't want to go on.

A storm was rising in her as she walked through those school
halls –
She just wanted to scream out to the world about what
happened –

Of what he did to her.

Then her knights in shining armor came,
But she soon found out they weren't really her knights.

She soon found out that they were ghouls, trolls, goblins and all
sorts of dark creatures in disguise –
They asked her:

"What were you wearing?
What did you do to cause this?
Did you approach him first?
Have you ever had sex before?
Do you have a boyfriend?
Is this a scheme for some revenge?"

They were dissecting her –
As if it wasn't bad enough –
What he had already done.

But what about him?

The only thing he had to say was if he was taking their deal or
not –
The only thing he had to hear was if he was innocent or guilty.

But no matter what the verdict, she would never feel like a
princess again.

No matter what happened to him, she would feel stuck in time as
if a curse was put upon her.

To live in her darkest moment,
When every touch felt like fire,
When she felt like she was being ripped apart from the inside out,
When she kicked and when she screamed –
And when she cried –
...For help.

Alone vs. Lonely

There's a difference between being alone and lonely

When you're alone
you are simply by yourself
enjoying yourself
expecting no company to come

When you're lonely
you could also be alone but
you don't always enjoy time by yourself
And you long for company

When you're alone, you can quickly have the thoughts of
another
Which leads you longing for them
yet leaving you able to bear the loneliness

When you're truly lonely
Your heart aches
And sometimes you can't help but cry
There are far too many thoughts crowding your mind

The constant battle is between alone and lonely

My constant battles between alone and lonely
Are because of you

Those constant thoughts of you are scattered throughout my
mind
Nothing else
No one else
Just you

How is this possible
To feel both alone and lonely

The two are so alike, yet
They're so different

… Like you

The Downfall to Being Myself

I love being myself.

I love to speak my mind.
- Telling the truth -
- Being blunt -
And being complex while still being my spunky
self.

But...
I don't actually *like* myself.

I don't like the fact that I scare some people
away.
I don't like it when I feel lonely,
or spend my nights crying.
I don't like that sometimes I don't have people to
spend time with -
that I have no one to share my emotions with.
And what sucks the most, is that...

Some people tell me to stay this way.

They tell me that-
I will soon attract people just like me -
That soon I won't be alone -
They say that it's great I'm always honest with
myself -
And they wish that-

They could be more like me.

Why?
Why would they want to be like me?

It's not all that great being me.
Not when there's nights I cry myself to sleep -
Not when there are days when I'm lonely -
And not when I scare some people away -
And certainly not when I hurt the ones I care
about the most.
So, if you ask me…

The greatest downfall to being myself-
is being myself.
Isn't it?...

Nicole Almengor is a sixteen-year-old junior at Piscataway High School. For Nicole, writing was always the way for her to deal with her emotions. And. over the years, her words blossomed into something far greater than just childhood diary entries. Not only is Nicole passionate about writing, but she also loves to draw, bake, read, watch anime, and play the ukulele. She creates her own comics and is also working toward opening her own bakery someday.

Nicole lives with her mother: Concetta, her Stepdad - Joe, little brother - Freddy, and two dogs - Mila and Simbad.

"Identity is a prison you can never escape, but the way to redeem your past is not to run from it, but try to understand it, and use it as a foundation to grow."

~Jay-Z

Shreya
Nilangekar

The Written Works
of
Shreya Nilangekar

"Imagination is more important than knowledge. Knowledge
is limited. Imagination encircles the world."

~Albert Einstein

Dreamcatcher

I'm a dream catcher
Sunshine tickles my feathers
Neurons turn into intricate patterns, cells into designs
Thinking? I don't think.
Anything that's left of my thoughts and feelings has been
replaced by one desire
One word, one purpose
One sound, one savior –
Spinning gold back into straw, and cobwebs to stars –
Dreams.

I'm breathing, but I'm not living
I'm waiting, but I'm not experiencing
I'm waiting to experience, living to breathe...
I'm waiting, waiting, waiting
Wanting, wanting, wanting
Ensnared in my web, dreams suffocating me like glass beads
Tightly coiled string, butterfly nets thrown out of my reach
The spinning wheel's spinning, but ambition sets the spindle
free...

The mind palace is exploding.
Vast like the ocean, but enclosed like the sea
Greed's got me fooled, I think I'm seeing too many dreams
Hourglasses broken, dangerous half-ideas floating around
Doubt lies in this nonsense, but I've already come this far along
It's time for me to pick an ending – Fate's singing the final song.

But my ending isn't necessarily *the* ending,
It's just a choice in the universe, a mere glint in my life
The truth is, I dream about more than I can handle
After all, when loneliness and power come into play
I have to do what I can so I won't go astray.

PROLOGUE

Lucas wanted to run away.

The decision was easy to make. Carrying it out was easier – or it should have been. He had wandered a little past his father's territory, occasionally stopping to drink water or to kill a hare. His pace, for some reason, never increased. It was as if he was treating the opportunity to run away as a casual walk.

Lucas never considered for a moment that he might not have wanted to leave. He knew leaving his pack would be hard, but his body seemed to refuse the action. His paws were already marking the light snow, creating tracks for him to remember his path home. As the land grew more and more unfamiliar, the hairs on his back rose. It was then that Lucas decided to stop.

It's simple, he thought, reassuring himself. *You just need to leave. There's no need to overthink it.*

But perhaps he had overthought his decision to leave. Lucas was not just any wolf. His large frame, covered by magnificent gray fur, and the saunter in his walk told that much. His crystal blue eyes, meant for attracting mates and dominating rival packs, shone in the moonlight. He had Alpha blood coursing through his veins.

Lucas's future was not his to choose. From the moment he was born, he had been training to prepare for his responsibilities as the Alpha. While his brothers and sisters were exploring new territory, still clinging to their mother's teats, Lucas was learning how to survive in the wild. His childhood was a series of marathons that never seemed to end. Each trial led to something more – whether it was approval from jealous uncles or skills that he would need as an adult wolf.

Lucas basked in the attention at first. He was always determined to be the strongest, smartest, and fastest wolf. Attracting females had never been difficult for him; an heir would be guaranteed. The entire pack, charmed by his diligence and abilities, offered him overwhelming support.

And just when he thought things could not get better, everything changed.

Suddenly, a tree branch snapped. Lucas turned around, ready to attack. He was surprised to see a young female wolf looking at him quietly, her head tilted to one side. She did not seem to be hiding the fact that she was staring at him, even though he had not noticed her presence. He found that odd. He had been trained to sense everything near him.

When he came closer to her, he realized that she had been looking at the sky intently, not at him. Her emerald eyes, focused on the landscape ahead of her, did not see him. She was a lanky wolf, her frail body and dirty white fur indicating that she had not lived the most luxurious of lives. He looked back at the trees in front of him and wondered what she found so interesting.

"Don't move." She said softly, her voice a contrast to her steely eyes. Lucas froze. "Let me enjoy the moment for a little longer."

Lucas tilted his head to the side, imitating her. He saw the moon casting its light over the trees, the darkness giving prey a place to hide. It had stopped snowing a while ago, but the cold wind remained relentless. The world seemed the same to him: accessible, and yet shrouded in mystery.

"What are you looking at?" Lucas asked after a minute had passed.

"I'm not looking," she answered, finally acknowledging his presence. Her gaze fixed on him, steely and cold. It seemed as if she was trying to appear detached and cool. Lucas felt slightly unnerved, but he did not show it. "I was feeling."

"Feeling what?"

"Feeling what it might have been like for my father to see his mate in this very moment." She said, sounding a little sad. "He met her on a night like this."

"Did you feel it?" Lucas asked. He thought he had seen her before in his pack, and he wondered why she was living so far away from their territory. He then remembered that only the most powerful of wolves lived near his father, and that a wolf like her was supposed to be considered average next to him.

"I don't feel anything." She admitted. "My father claimed that she was shining like the sun when he was first met her. I wanted to see if I could feel it here."

"I don't believe in mates." Lucas said. "Are you from my pack?"

"Alpha Adrian's son?" she asked. He nodded. The title, which once filled him with pride, rang emptily in the air. "I thought I might have seen you before."

"My name is Lucas." The wolf said, hoping she would understand what he wanted to be called.

"I'm Mina." Mina said, but she was distracted. "Why don't you believe in mates?"

"Why do you?" Lucas asked. "We're wolves, not humans. How can we fall in love?"

"I never said I believed in love. The pack tells us we're supposed to fall in love so we don't kill each other. Just like how the pack says that wolf gods created this earth for wolves to live in." Mina said sarcastically.

"You don't believe in love or God, but you believe in mates?" Lucas mused. "Does that mean you believe that crescent moons appear on our foreheads when we meet our mates?"

Mina looked surprisingly calm. "I don't believe in the pack's version of love or God. But that doesn't mean that there isn't something. There's a reason why *every single wolf* says they've seen a crescent moon before."

Lucas scoffed. "Mating is culture. Culture is how our pack has survived for so long. Crescent moons and mates are just ways to make life more interesting."

"Are you sure you're supposed to be Alpha? You don't sound like one."

"I'm not going to be Alpha," Lucas declared. "I'm leaving this pack. For good."

Mina did not react in the way he thought she would. She seemed distant, as if she were lost in her own world. "The pack says that gods created a world only for wolves to live in, but we protect ourselves from humans. The pack says that mates exist, but there's no proof. I understand why you would want to leave the pack."

"You don't know anything about me." Lucas said, surprised at the bitter tone that came out of him. "You don't know why I want to leave."

136

"I think I do know why you want to leave." Mina said, her emerald eyes blazing. "Don't think I haven't felt it either. Life's easier when you see things the way you want to see them. But the moment it starts to get complicated, you want to leave."

"That's not why I want to leave," Lucas insisted, but he felt her words impacting him in some way. He wondered how two sentences could say something that had taken him years to realize. "I see things exactly the way they are. There's no place for me here."

A silence fell over them. The night had begun to get darker. Lucas thought of the things that might wait for him at the end of the forest if he chose to leave. But if he chose to stay, he would have to accept a future that would make him unhappy. There was a certain solace that Lucas took in uncertainty that he did not take in unhappiness.

Lucas had started to walk away when Mina began to speak again. "Leaving won't make a difference. Maybe you'll find a new place to stay or a new pack to belong to. But the moment life changes, you'll be gone again. You can avoid being Alpha, but you can't avoid change."

"Are you calling me a coward?" Lucas demanded, seething. His head spun. One minute she had appeared calm, the next minute foolish, the minute after that annoying. He did not understand why he was still talking to her.

"I'm telling you that life will change. You will change. One day, you will find your mate." Mina's breaths were coming out in gasps, as if she was finally telling him what she really wanted to say. "And if she dies before you do, you'll tell stories about your undying love for her, even if you've never actually loved her."

"I would never do that." Lucas said, disgusted. He had never understood what love was, or what it was supposed to look like. Did love continue through old age as his parents claimed it did, even though they barely talked to each other anymore? Or was it something one could sense at first sight, like the female wolf he had met days before said?

"My father was never in love with my mother," Mina rambled on. "But the moment she died, he loved her until his last days. It's a curse, I think, but the pack never mentioned anything about *that*."

Lucas wanted to ask why she was telling him this, but thought better of it. The pack would realize he was gone soon enough, and he would not be able to escape in time. The thought sobered him.

"I'm leaving. Pretend you never saw me here." He said, walking away swiftly. Mina was eerily silent. He felt her eyes follow his footsteps, her gaze penetrating him.

"Do you know how female wolves spot their mates?" Mina yelled. Lucas ignored her and kept on walking. He suddenly felt as if he would never leave. He walked faster.

"We dream about meeting them!" she shouted. Then her voice lowered. "I thought maybe you'd shine like the sun, too."

Lucas stopped in his tracks.

When he turned around, he saw a crescent moon carved on Mina's forehead, ending every dream he ever had for himself.

* * * * *

THE LEGEND OF SCARLET THE WOLF

The winter had taken a toll on him, for a wolf his age had difficulty surviving such harsh winters. His once handsome features were washed away along with his magnificent gray fur, now clinging to a somewhat frail body. The only reminder of what he could have been was the crescent moon on his forehead that shone under the starry night.

The wolf known as Scarlet sniffed into the snow hesitantly, his paw prints vanishing into the ice that covered the ground like a blanket. His crystal blue pupils narrowed into tiny slits as he inspected the area for the scent of a wild animal. Only days before he had pounced on a hare mercilessly and tore it apart, his bloodlust taking over him as the warm blood trickled down his chin. Now the only thing the old wolf craved was warmth and a sense of security from the bitter cold.

He looked up at the moonless sky, remembering a night like this one. Scarlet's heart throbbed with a dull ache, a dark stone falling over his chest. On nights like this, Scarlet thought of his lost mate and mourned her death. The empty memories haunted his

138

every waking moment and chased his dreams. The scar, which had never healed over time, was still fresh.

He had memorized every detail of her face, in fear of letting her features erode from his mind. She had been the only female to catch his eye, back when he was young and foolish. As soon as he had laid his eyes on her, he knew she had to be his. Scarlet was amused at her bold, rebellious spirit that had shocked everyone else. He almost snickered at what he had to do to prove his love for her.

The day she confessed her love for him was the day she made another sacrifice – her life. When Scarlet closed his eyes, he could see her emerald eyes shining with tears, a look of sadness and relief on her face.

I love you, she had whispered. *And I have never loved you more than I do in this moment. Remember, my dear, that my love will always go beyond the afterlife.*

The wolf had thrown his head back and howled, his screams of agony piercing the air. For what was and what could have been. His childish fantasies were ruined, no, *murdered,* in one moment. In the hands of Fate, the one thing he had ever believed in, lay the blood of his future children and a life with Mina he would never be able to have.

The first days after Mina's death were the most painful. After burying her body with the traditional rituals, he had bid his clan farewell. A wolf was nothing without his clan, but it was only the nothingness in his bones that Scarlet could feel. He had no aim, no purpose, the self-blame consuming his core. When that passed, the temptation for revenge ignited in his heart. It burned intensely, giving him motivation to survive.

His to-be mate was murdered by the alpha of an enemy clan, known as the formidable Leon. The day their bond was going to be completed, Leon challenged Scarlet to a duel to fight for his mate. Scarlet accepted, and a dangerous fight ensued. Snarling, biting, spewing blood, and the tearing of limbs were witnessed by the full moon that hung above them.

Just as Scarlet assured himself of his victory, about to howl in glory, Leon attacked him at the last minute. Closing his eyes, Scarlet had expected his defeat and his sudden death. That had been his biggest mistake.

What Scarlet had not expected was his lifeless mate on the ground, blood gushing out of the deep scratches meant for Scarlet. Her last words echoed in his mind. As she took her last breath, Scarlet made a final vow: to avenge her death.

Leon and his clan had mysteriously disappeared after the tragic incident. Scarlet spent fifteen torturous years tracking them down, eliminating the members, and killing all their descendants. Consumed by destruction and rage, he did not rest until his mission was complete. He showed no mercy and did not listen to anyone.

Soon enough, rumors began to spread of an independent wolf causing havoc. This earned him the nickname Scarlet, The Wolf who lived to kill and destroy, always covered in the scent of blood. Scarlet ignored these rumors and held his head up high, daring anyone to challenge him. Only few were stupidly brave to try to steal his newfound power.

And yet, when he had killed those young wolves, he saw himself inside of them.

Leon's death had been everything Scarlet trained for. Once they had met again, Scarlet did not hesitate during the battle. As he tore Leon's head off, the relief was fleeting, replaced by pain again. Revenge, as Scarlet had learned, was bittersweet.

Now he wandered into nowhere, like the first days after Mina's death.

Suddenly Scarlet collapsed, his body numb with cold. His teeth chattered but he refused to let something so insignificant get to him. He tried to get up but to no avail; the ripping sensation in his bones told him he could no longer move. His physical fragility struck him for the first time, and Scarlet realized how close he was to Death.

Food was scarce in the winter. Wolves usually found caves to hibernate in for shelter and warmth. Scarlet had no such luck; the endless snow on the ground showed nothing in sight. Now he had hit his limit. This was how he was going to die, alone and miserable, surrendering to the hands of Nature.

So be it, he thought. *So I will die. It was going to come eventually.* He shut his eyes and waited for Death to take him into the night.

140

But Death did not come. The wolf did not understand. Was this a form of punishment for his crimes and the sinful life he had led after the loss of his mate? Did he truly deserve this? He waited for what seemed like ages, but Death teased him.

The frustration turned into pain. Real and raw, it clawed at his body and deep into his bones. He screamed into nothing, the dark void he had concealed for so many years erupting into different emotions. He lay paralyzed in the snow, his heart beating irregularly. Tears streamed down his face, revealing the depth of his sadness and depression.

When Scarlet closed his eyes, blinded by tears, he was there again, trapped. Leon was running toward him, murderous rage in his eyes, reaching for Scarlet's throat. Scarlet tensed, waiting, noticing the oddly bent branch sticking out of the tree behind him. If Leon came close enough and Scarlet moved out of the way, maybe –

Mina lay there bleeding, the crescent moon on her forehead flickering. Scarlet felt the life drain out of her body, the mating process being reversed, an ending for her but a new path for him.

The fear in Leon's eyes, but that hardly mattered at the moment -

"You didn't listen to me." Mina said, but her eyes betrayed her fear of dying. "My foolish mate, what have you done?"

Scarlet fumbled for an apology, trying to think of something to say, but Mina bridged the gaps for them. Her love confession, something that was supposed to be done with love, was stained with blood and injustice. Why had she wasted her breath on him, a wolf who could not even protect his mate?

The infant sky, cleared of stars, mocked him. This was the fate of his relationship with Mina. He would always come back here, reliving the moment again and again. A love that had never grown, a love that had never matured beyond his pride and hasty decision making -

The rumors, Scarlet thought, *Leon warned me well enough of his arrival.*

I did this to myself. I did this to myself -

Scarlet opened his eyes, gasping for breath. Nightmares…were they nightmares or were they reality? Dark spots appeared in his vision, his brain fighting to survive. Scarlet laughed mirthlessly to the empty air. He laughed so hard his fragile bones ached. The realization of how old he was caused him to laugh harder.

"Lucas…" a familiar voice echoed.

His ears perked up at his real name, his lost identity. He was imagining. She wasn't here. She was dead, just as dead he was inside.

"Mina…" he uttered her name after what had felt like centuries. He closed his eyes, her name flooding his being with relief and love. Love, pure love without the heartache and agony, was what he felt for her. Mina was his first and last love in his lifetime.

The picture of Mina floated from the back of his mind. He could see her clearly now. She was there, painfully real, standing above him with an amused grin on her face. Her white fur began to glow an ethereal blue, eyes illustrating the love and kindness he had missed over the years. She was so beautiful, the very image of a wolf goddess.

"Mina…" he managed to grunt. "Take me with you…"

Mina chuckled, her laugh like tinkling bells. She burned so brightly that he should have shielded his eyes, but he couldn't. Looking away from her was such a difficult task. He drank in her appearance, her beauty, finally seeing what he had dreamt about for so long.

Mina leaned down and giggled. She began to lick his face affectionately like she used to. Scarlet sighed and enjoyed the feeling of being loved again. He felt his wounds being mended, giving him the energy to stand up again and join her.

"Mina." He commanded, his voice gruff. "Let me join you."

Mina winked. "Follow me, love." She whispered.

She didn't have to say it twice. They ran together, white and gray blurs invisible in the darkness. He felt his limbs moving again, free of pain. He was happy again, and he was with Mina. They would be together now for eternity, with nothing to ruin the ending they should have had.

They reached a steep precipice, the icicles glinting in the night. He looked at her, confused. Mina nudged him and stepped toward the edge, signaling him to follow her. Scarlet froze, feeling fear for the first time.

"Come," Mina told him softly.

Scarlet looked at her beautiful features, never wanting to disappoint her again. He had never felt surer of anything in his life. Mina stepped over the cliff, her being fading away into the sky.

Without hesitation, Scarlet flung himself over the cliff, filled with happiness and delight. His body landed painfully hard, his bones cracking and his body bleeding profusely. Nothing else mattered but Mina. He rose, surprised the fall didn't kill him, and left a trail of fresh blood on the snow as he limped.

He would join her into the afterlife at any cost. It was just a matter of how long he would survive.

"Mina, I'm coming!" Scarlet yelled.

THE END

Paper Petals

Three years ago
I pitied the daises I ruined.
If I'd really been in love,
I would have wished for a garden of dandelions
instead of plucking the petals clean from their roots,
destroying every single dream I had.

But what's there to mourn if the petals were meant to be ashes
Scattered, gray, deceiving
Burning like flimsy paper for the "love" I once had.

What's there to mourn if the flowers grew into prickly thorns
Picking at me relentlessly,
refusing to become roses.
What's there to mourn if I never had a garden in the first place?

I still think about it three years later
because the roots never grew back strong enough –
I don't know where to plant myself.
The soil I stand on is no longer mine, after all
It's not mine if I've let other people make it for me
because I couldn't do it myself.

I'm here now, wondering if I'm destined for a garden or a
wasteland
Wondering why I haven't noticed the comets before
Flying, exploding into stardust
landing among the stars.
I've looked down so much that I've never really seen the sky before
Never seen the freedom it could hold.

The sky's the limit, I've been told
But for me, it's just a starting point.
What's there to mourn if the paper petals were created to burn,
allowing me to notice the stars instead?
What's there to mourn if the paper petals were made of stardust all
along – unfit to live in a place where they weren't meant to exist.

Shreya Nilangekar is a junior at Piscataway High School. She has always dreamed of living in a magical, fantastical world, and creating one is something she plans to make a reality. Shreya has always enjoyed writing poems and short stories, but her real dream is to showcase her soul to the world in the form of her written works. In the meantime, you can find Shreya critiquing books and movies, playing the violin, and daydreaming about what is certain to be a beautiful future.

"Living is easy with eyes closed –
misunderstanding all you see."

~John Lennon

The Written Works
of
Zahraa Shaikh

"Let your love be stronger than your hate or anger.
Learn the wisdom of compromise,
for it is better to bend a little than to break."

~H.G. Wells

Reflection

When some people see themselves in the mirror
Immediately they think they're not good enough
Either for themselves, or others, or for the world.

They think they're ugly.
They think they're fat.
They think that no one will ever love them.

Well, let me tell you -
Everything you just said to yourself is wrong!
You're only saying that because some other person with a
negative personality and their own ugly self-image said it
to you, or about you.
Don't ever listen to them!
They're not worth it.
They don't know a thing about what's really beautiful.

What matters is that -
You are beautiful in your own way, every day, and in every
way!
Continue to be your beautiful self.
You're fabulous!
Continue to be your fabulous self! – always
Don't ever change for someone else
It's not worth it to lose who you are.
Be true, and fabulous, and beautiful.
Be **you.**

My Life With My Best Friend

My life is beautiful
My life is sweet and awesome
And, it's all because you're my best friend.

I'm glad for you to be yourself,
To be such a good person,
Because, that's good for me, too.
That's why you will always be my best friend!

You are: understanding, caring, friendly, funny,
wonderful, compassionate, creative, and so much
more.

I could never find anyone else like you.
I could never, ever replace you.
Thank you for always being here for me.

I have all the love and all the caring I need right
here and right now - because of you.
You are truly my best friend - for life!

Nature

The sun is shining
The sky is refining
The grass is displaying its bright, green colors
The birds are singing
The flowers are blooming

How beautiful nature is!

On days like this I love to spend time with nature
With this thought alone I realize that
nature is something we should all care for and protect
This is why I help nature along in any way that I can
For I am a part of the world too.

Nature is…
Wonderful
Beautiful
Inspiring

I hope you will join those like me
And help **to k**eep nature safe, beautiful, and strong.

Give Nature some of its love back.

~~~

Depression

It sucks when you have depression
Life becomes very hard for you

All the hobbies you love to do
Turn into things you start to hate

You have terrible thoughts
You feel like there's no point to life anymore

No matter how much you try to be happy
You're still not satisfied with your life

You start to have a battle with yourself
Then the voices in your head become demons you're
fighting, too

Will you win or lose?
Will it really matter if you **never** change?
IF you never change, you will remain the same **before,
during** and **after** every single fight.

STOP!

You need to realize:
There **are** people you can to talk to
There **are** people who will listen.
There **are** people who can help you.
Reach out!
Tell them how you feel!

They'll help you until you are your best and healthiest self!
My gentle advice to you is this:

Keep going and never give up!
I believe in you.
Others believe in you.

You can do it!

I know you can.
We know you can.
Just never give up.

Never, never, ever give up on **you!**

Zahraa

Zahraa Naveed Shaikh is a seventeen-year-old girl attending Piscataway High School. She is in eleventh grade.

Zahraa is an energetic, caring, open-minded, determined, and generous person. She meets hardships head-on and doesn't allow the past to hold her down. Zahraa is forever optimistic about her future. She also helps others when they go through their own hard times. She helps them in any way possible. She's a happy spirit.

Zahraa currently lives with her loving family: Mohammad NaveedShaikh, Shazia Shaikh, Ammaarah Shaikh, Ruqiyyah Shaikh, and, Mohammad Abdurrahman Shaikh.

She is the middle child in the family. She loves having such a large, wonderful family. They are the heart of her existence.

When Zahraa graduates college, she wants to become a graphic designer.

"There are two basic motivating forces: fear and love. When we are afraid, we pull back from life. When we are in love, we open to all that life has to offer with passion, excitement, and acceptance."

~John Lennon

The Written Works
of
Aisha Humaira

"I like nonsense, it wakes up the brain cells.
Fantasy is a necessary ingredient in living."

~Dr. Seuss

__Mistakes__

Sparkling eyes and hearts of crystal,
Polished to perfection, timeless miracles,
Finished puzzles, we are born to fly,
Only to be shot down for soaring too high.
Suffocated for daring to breathe,
Handcuffed for trying to spread our wings openly.

It's a war zone where we always seem to lose,
Where pathological liars pose as tellers of truth.
And we delude ourselves for the sake of company,
Why is it that people damage each other so severely?
Why are betrayal and hurt so prominent in our nature?
Why do we inflict these on each other and wait for karma
to catch up later?
Because even friends disappoint unlike the way of enemies.
Trust no one and maintain your own army,
Have no expectations and you'll suffer no disappointments,
But hoping for better next time seems to be part of our
temperament.
How many tries does it take,
Before realizing getting so close was the biggest mistake?

Promises made and words said are sometimes only for the
instant,
And when we reflect on them years later their meaning is
nonexistent.

It's hard to know if you're hurting someone unconsciously.
I'd rather preserve my pride and stay silent if I'm sinking,
I'd rather drown gracefully.
Because people are only temporary,
And a hand lent can be just as quickly withdrawn,
Contemplated for just a moment before moving on.

Hours of conversation on end can mean the world
Until months later when you fade without a word,
This ability to jump from one person to the next,
It's an ability with which I have not been blessed.
I've found it's best to detach myself from it all,
Because by getting too close,
you're only building yourself up to fall

And break, because people break each other.
We're dynamite, destructive by nature.
I never really understood it, and I doubt I ever will.
I remain unusually still, silently glum like raindrops on a
window sill.
I guess the clouds never really go away.
When you're battling the faults of human nature,
They tend to stay.

We shoot arrows at each other, then question why we
bleed.
We hammer into glass and blame the fragility of the piece.
We shove each other aside,
Face-first into oceans of contempt, watch each other drown

And blame the rushing of the tide.
We damage each other without being aware of it,
Yet the ignorance never lessens the pain of the hit.
And once a heart begins to bleed, it doesn't clot so soon,
It writhes in agony before dwelling in the solitude it has
grown accustomed to.

Mentally distance yourself where no one can reach you,
Give yourself the lessons that no one can teach you,
Because even your own shadow leaves you in the dark,
So why take a look around to begin with,
Discover the emptiness, and let it leave a mark?
Because people are temporary despite what they say,
I like to believe otherwise, yet
We are all left with our own hand to hold
at the very end of the day.

Amnesia

I long for the feeling
To not feel at all
To build a barrier around myself
And remain secure within its walls

What does it take to be indifferent
To let life itself pass by
With not the slightest emotion, care, thought
Or blink of an eye

I wonder if it's possible to erase
Years at a time, the way I fell
Face-down, in pieces
So broken I could hardly recognize myself

I wish to empty my mind
So its contents are flushed away
Like the rubbish they are
Deepening wounds that are waiting to fade

Doused in poison and sputtering
Tongue still bitter and heart in despair
I've fallen victim to the toxicity of desire
And damaged myself beyond repair

How ungrateful I must seem
With my petty whims and heart of stone

But tell me how can you judge
A story you've never been told

I've been fading in fragments, this recklessly
outgoing spirit
Of which they were all so fond
It won't be long now
Going…
Going…
gone.

<u>Colors</u>

They're all so devoid of color,
Life's a black and white movie.
But I guess you could say I'm soaked in a kaleidoscope,
Drenched in everything that's ever happened to me.

It's a burning red like the passion I once had and lost,
Or like the blood spilled in every mental battle I waged,
Dripping into puddles of love and hate,
Trickling on to this once-empty page.

Radiating a tranquility I have yet to learn,
Is the muted orange like a faint sunset's glow.
Beautiful in essence, while I'm a mess of neon,
Too dynamic to be followed.

Golden like every beautiful day I've let slip
Unnoticed, bursts of inspiration and peace of mind,
Golden like the anticipated pot of gold at the end of each
rainbow,
I've tried to travel across and have yet to find.

It's green with the envy I've so often fallen victim to,
Like every insecurity I've kept boarded up
Under lock and key,
An enemy I like to keep hushed.

And it's a dreary blue haze, raindrops slipping
Down a car window, tears carving their tracks.
It's nostalgia, a remarkable race with time,
The cold shoulder when begging to turn it back.

It's a vibrant purple, alive and electric,
Untamed in ways I should be by now.
A stubborn spirit, an irrepressible energy,
I'm working on containing, though I'm still unsure how.

Jet black like the web of lies I've spun,
Like the deceit and uncontrolled offenses I've spoken,
I never claimed to be a saint in the slightest,
But here's to the promises I've kept unbroken.

And here's to the transparent being,
I know I'll never be.
Crystal clear with a mind whose shallow waters,
Are easy to tread and complexity-free.

A mosaic of color and intensity,
Not all the pieces fit perfectly,
I'm still puzzling over
What the picture's supposed to be.

Like the rainbow blended on a child's fingertips,
It's splattered paint on a canvas, roughly mixed hues.
A colorful mind that's gotten a taste of everything,
A spectrum that has a tendency to speak too soon.

And it's these unfiltered colors,
And impossibly loud spirit that I can't keep restrained.
I'm leaving vivid footprints in my wake,
Hoping my colors are strong enough to never fade.

Aisha Humaira is a seventeen-year-old senior at Piscataway High School. She has had a passion for writing ever since she was a child and has continued it as a hobby throughout middle school and high school. She specifically enjoys writing poetry about her personal experiences and has kept a journal of them for the past eight years. Aisha is an only child who is also interested in the STEM field, potentially as a career, and balances it with her love for the arts. Aside from writing, Aisha enjoys reading, listening to music, and hanging out with friends and family.

"Looking back over a lifetime, you see that love was the answer to everything."

~Ray Bradbury

The Written Works
of
Elijah DiGirolamo

"The oldest and strongest emotion of mankind is fear.
And the oldest and strongest kind of fear
is the fear of the unknown…"

~H.P. Lovecraft

The Ruins Outside Fallwich

The mighty howl of the wind screamed through the cold night. A storm was brewing. The young man walked across the busy street - ignoring oncoming vehicles. The drivers in the cars appeared to him as mere high beams, beeping horns loudly, pressing their hands to extend the noise.

Thomas quickly climbed over the guardrail and into the forest which surrounded the quaint town of Fallwich, New Jersey.

From deep within his pockets, he pulled out a small box of matches and sat on a fallen tree, now bridging a creek. Thomas ripped out a match and struck it upward, spawning a flickering, orange flame. He reached for his old-fashioned lantern and quickly lit it, creating an even brighter and much needed source of light. Thomas blew out the match and then threw the cold, blackened stick into the darkness. The lantern, which he held by the grip, made everything around him visible. The orange light revealed herds of doe and fawn, that instantly ran out of sight. Thomas trudged his way through the thick, tall grass, and made a quick bound over a small stream. A tiny frog leapt away, frightened by Thomas' presence as he jumped over the water. In the light of day, the forest was the apotheosis of natural beauty, but at night, it was a nexus of extreme nightmares.

The menacing hoots of owls, a chorus of crickets, and the rustling of leaves were sounds that echoed in the dreadful night. An earthy aroma that permeated throughout the woods was also present.

Fallwich was a heavily populated suburban town, but the outer cores were a completely different story, especially at night. Thomas pressed on into the guts of the forest in search of a legendary, ancient house, which stood tall on a hill, looming over both Piscataway and Fallwich. He wanted to prove himself among his peers at school, who constantly gossiped about the mythic building. "**No one would wanna go in there! No way! Not for all the tea in the China!**" Many of his peers maintained.

"**I will.**" Thomas vowed.

164

In return, he received shocked looks from the faces of the teens around him. One of the bigger kids stood up. "**Yeah? Then bring us somethin' back from the house to prove it! And do it at night!**" The big kid dared.

Thomas smugly answered, "**Challenge accepted.**"

Admittedly, Thomas was nervous to go out into the woods of Fallwich at night, but he was determined to come out victorious among the people at school. He walked carefully to prevent the loud crunching of dry leaves on the grassy floor. He moved his arm, slightly, guiding the light of the lantern here and there to see things more clearly. After a few seconds of walking, something caught his eye. In the light, he noticed a shoe on the ground, lying next to some twigs and leaves. He took a closer look at it and realized it was a horribly-bloodied sneaker, torn completely apart by what appeared to be razor sharp claws. He gulped as a sense of dread overwhelmed him. For some reason, he thought of the legend of the Jersey Devil, a story about a winged creature that roamed the Pine Barrens of southern New Jersey. Then, Thomas took a deep breath, believing that maybe a raccoon or a fox had used the shoe as a chew-toy. He never believed in the supernatural, but the thoughts of it frightened him. As he convinced himself that it may have been an animal, a flurry of provocative questions floated through his mind.

Where did the shoe come from? Who did it belong to? Did the owner of the shoe make it out of the woods *alive*? Thomas produced an unwelcomed sigh as he walked by the torn sneaker. That was followed by the words, "**What the hell did I get myself into?**"

After a few more minutes of treading through the dark woods, he stumbled upon a 1950s pickup truck. It was rusted all over, it had no wheels, and the hood was opened slightly. An artifact from the past, he thought. As he moved in closer to the vehicle, Thomas noticed that all the windows were completely covered in dust. And, on the front windshield was a recently smeared, finger-written warning of sorts. The scribbled message read, "NO ESCAPE." The eerie cautioning chilled Thomas to the bone as he stood closer to the window, nearer the driver's seat. The window was blanketed in so much dust that he couldn't see anything within the vehicle. Thomas used his free hand to wipe the grime from the glass and then, he shined his lantern inside the truck. He gasped and jumped backward. There, in front of him, was an aged skeleton sitting in the driver's seat, staring right back at him, its mouth wide-open. Thomas continued to flee, lantern in hand, far away from the truck. So horribly shaken, he unknowingly bolted deeper into the woods, ending up on a steep hill, which was safeguarded by numerous dead trees. Sweat ran down his terror-stricken face as he looked over the woods at the top of the hill. Then, with a somber tone, he murmured, "**How could I *ever* think this was a good idea? I'm SUCH an idiot!**"

He then turned around to find the old house.

A lightning strike, the first of the storm, illuminated the mansion in blue. The structure was desolate, complete with boarded up windows, rotting wood, and mossy gargoyles watching from above.

Thomas was understandably fearful at the sight of the mansion, for it measured at an enormous height and had a frightful appearance akin to something straight out of an Edgar Allan Poe story. The ominous rumbling of thunder didn't help the situation either. Regardless, Thomas arrogantly cheered to himself, "**I did it! I freakin' did it!**"

He hesitated for a moment, and then made his way up the small steps of the grand portico. The gray, rotting wood cracked underneath Thomas' hiking boots before he made it to the front door. He twisted the ornate, rusted doorknob and entered the forgotten house. The door opened in hesitance, and made a long and groaning sound. Thomas shined his lantern to look inside.

Immediately, he noticed a somewhat barren living room, complete with a partially missing staircase. Thomas reluctantly entered the cobweb-infested room. The first floorboard he stepped on squeaked loudly, creating a menacing echo throughout the abandoned house. He looked around, noticing many types of generations-old furniture. He felt a bit more confident now that he was finally inside the house, where so many stories had swirled around town for decades.

There were urban legends about it being haunted, rumors of devil worship, and other occult happenings. And now, it appeared as if none of those accounts were true.

But his sense of bravery quickly turned to dismay when he heard a strange noise emanate from a nearby hallway. It sounded something like feet squashing their way through mud.

Then, slowly, Thomas turned his head toward the direction of the sound. A chill spread throughout his entire body as he saw the silhouette of an unnatural figure, making rapid, twitching, and volatile movements, all-the-while creating that horrifying noise. Thomas stood frozen, staring at the black figure. He couldn't tell what it was. But he had to know. The curiosity got the best of him and he shined the lantern toward the corridor. He weakly gasped and stumbled backward. The orange light revealed a hulking canine face'd creature, with a sinister grin among bloodied fangs. Another bolt of lightning from outside revealed black goatish horns atop the beast's head and enormous, partly closed, leathery-looking wings attached to bulky shoulders. The monster's skin was grey with the rough texture of an elephant. Vilest of all, in its muscular hands, it held a fresh, headless upper body, intestines dangling in strings. Suddenly, a bloody white shoe fell toward the stairway. The twin to the other shoe, that Thomas had found in the woods, an hour earlier.

Adding further terror to the grisly sight, the creature hissed incessantly, in a din that was ungodly.

Scared half to death, Thomas fell onto the weakened floor's foundation, and within seconds, it broke beneath him, causing the floor to open up into a wide, gaping hole. Thomas fell through it, wounding himself on the sharp wooden splinters.

He landed in a cavernous chamber. The ground, beneath him, felt soft and sandy. Thomas was terrified and in tremendous pain. He held his injured arm close to his body as he dragged his feet along the ground. The gargoyle-like beast was still fresh in his mind, keeping Thomas entrenched in his ever-present sense of endangerment. He was even more petrified when he realized his lantern was missing! Thomas panicked. He lost his footing and fell yet again onto more sandy ground. Suddenly, his body began to sink into the silt and grit. In a desperate attempt at survival he grabbed hold of a rocky wall, and climbed up to safety. As he pulled himself upward, a rotting, skeletal arm reached out and clawed at his jeans. Thomas screamed in terror as he kicked the arm backward.

The rancid smell of decaying flesh now permeated the cave.

A skull, attached to ribs and a sternum, suddenly rose from the sand, moaning, "**Save… Us…**"

Thomas jumped over the skeleton, frenetically powering himself through the sand as even more hands grabbed at him, slashing open parts of his jeans with their sharp and jagged claws. Thomas escaped within an inch of his life from the pool of swarming, and unrelenting skeletons.

Despite the madness, he found a narrow tunnel to his immediate left and ran straight through it - the ghostly voices still at his back.

Tears streamed down Thomas' face as he ran through a rock-strewn corridor, toward a hope-filled freedom.

Suddenly, he hit a dead end.

Pained and despairing, Thomas pressed his hands against his face and sobbed, "**I knew it! I knew I shouldn't have come here!**"

Those words had barely left his lips when a metallic object crashed onto the floor in front of him. "**My lantern!!!**"

Thomas frantically reached into his pockets **"Matches! Where the hell are my matches?!!!**"

Incredibly, *miraculously*, the matches appeared, and the lantern was lit!

But Thomas' hope was short-lived, as the lamplight revealed an encroaching army of skeletal figures.

One stood out above the others.

It was a tall skeleton, with spiraling horns protruding from the top of its skull, making it appear even taller. Its eyes glowed an ill-omened red under the darkness of his hooded shroud. Thomas screamed and shrieked as he slid back on the floor, as far away from the specter as he possibly could.

Nevertheless, the entity reached out for Thomas, piercing the flesh of his cheeks with its razor-sharp talons.

And, with a look of wicked satisfaction and finality, it uttered these words -

"**Welcome… Home….**"

168

The Vigilante

"Sooner or later, if man is ever to be worthy of his destiny, we must fill our hearts with tolerance." ~Stan Lee

Ever since I was a little kid, I have always had a distinct fascination with horror and the occult. My dad called me a freak for liking that kind of stuff, which is just one of the reasons my mom filed for divorce so early in my childhood. The things he said to me, even though long ago, still affect me - even if in a small way. And so, because of that, books and movies have always been an escape for me. And, now more than ever, I'm drawn into that horror film/occult genre. They pulled me into the world of fantasy and cleared out the negativity from the real world. As scary as it may seem, it all felt safe to me. And, throughout those lonely and semi-escapist childhood years and preschool years, my mom raised me. And she was a good and caring mother. She did all she could to support me, through my good times and bad times, as well as through her own good times and bad times. I clearly recall receiving a book for my seventh birthday. It was a rather large hardcover containing a brilliant collection of stories by Edgar Allan Poe, and it stood to reinforce my appreciation for that genre. Ever since then, I've collected a great number of those horror novels and movies.

As years moved on and I was in my teens, it appeared that my semi-isolation made me a social outcast of sorts. As a junior in high school, I was often seen alone with a book in my hand, or reading at lunchtime, or in homeroom. I had branched out into Stephen King and Dean Koontz, among many others by then. And, annually, I would re-read my Edgar Allan Poe collection since the tales and visuals that came with them were timeless to me. And, while my home life was quite good that year, school was very polarizing, and it was far scarier to me than any movie I have seen or story I have read. Real life usually is.

But I wasn't expecting what transpired. And it started in a mid-morning Chemistry class. First off, it was a subject I didn't particularly excel in, no matter how hard I'd try. The class was small - six people, including me. The work didn't bother me, even though, as I said, I was no Chemistry Wizard. What did bother me were the people. Two guys in particular whose blasphemous names I shudder at mentioning: Joshua Robertson and Martin Cooper, an 'undynamic' duo of unsavory proportion. They were the type of guys who felt that by acting cool, that they really were cool. But no really 'cool' guys would ever live their lives in the way Josh and Marty did. All they did was label their mean, aggressive, arrogance as "cool." And I didn't know anyone who was safe from their abuses. They even gave our teacher, Mrs. Fields, a rough time when he was trying so hard to do her job. They threw pencils, papers, and their ignorance around the room. Then, they decided they needed a more significant target.

I was doing problems on my worksheet and to the side of my desk, my Edgar Allan Poe book rested. I listened to classical rock music as I did my work, but something didn't feel right to me. I felt anxious and I had nervous butterflies in my stomach. I paused my music. The second the music stopped I heard the staged laughter of Joshua and Martin, a few desks away from me. It was unsettling to hear, but I had no idea why... Until I heard what they were saying.

"Look at this ass-****! HEY! You like scary sh*t? We got some scary for ya. Would you and 'Edgar' like that?! Wouldja, Big Boy?" Joshua pushed.

I quickly looked around the room, scanning everyone's desk. I was trying to convince myself that they were talking about someone else, not me. My brief investigation concluded when I saw no one else with a book on their desk, nonetheless someone with another Edgar Allan Poe book. Sweat started to run down my face as I succumbed to an anxious kind of heat that spread throughout my body. I bit my lip nervously, trying to re-focus on my work. But, Marty picked up where Josh left off. "HEY! My friend asked you a question, ****-head! You got the balls to handle that, Big Boy?! Or are ya too scared to be *really* scared?!" I watched as Martin pounded his fist into his other hand. "You see this!?"

His blatant offense was followed by Joshua's cackle, one he frequently enjoyed by imitating a classic Halloween witch. At this point, I felt very insecure and defenseless. I mustered the courage to move my eyes in their direction. Then, I was victim to a hideous sight. They were looking at me with wide, toothy grins that pierced my soul, saying more malicious things about me, ridiculing me, doing all they could to break my spirit.

Mrs. Fields stood by, helplessly. And, with the exception of dismissing the class, and asking me to remain seated, none of the angst I felt was alleviated - not one bit.

And the "cool guys" laughter continued in the hallway.

The next few days got even worse.

On Wednesday, I caught them again, making fun of me. Marty was the first to start. "What trashcan didja get those sneakers out of?"

"You get your lunch outta trash cans too, Big Boy?" Martin's remarks came one after the other, as if he had nothing better to do.

Joshua giggled like a mental patient, "He's a loser and a reject!" Marty then unleashed his creepy imitation of Jack Nicholson's "The Shining" smile. It was one thing after the next, and I was getting sick of it. I tried to get myself together, but I came up short at every turn. Even when I went home and was inside a safe place, I couldn't eat my dinner, and I had a rough night sleeping. That evening I felt as hopeless and restless as the day I just had. Thank God I didn't have class with them on Thursday, but, what did it matter, their voices still haunted me.

Friday was, by far, the worst day of the entire week. My last period was Chemistry and I wanted to cut class, but I didn't feel right doing that. So, I walked in looking calm and serene, which was nothing close to what I was feeling on the inside. All I wanted was for the time to pass quickly. I tried my best to ignore Joshua and Martin by listening to some loud rock music, but it only made the situation worse. Whatever it was they were saying, I couldn't resist hearing, so I paused my music, which I immediately regretted. "Hear that? Now he thinks he's a heavy metal badass!" Martin spilled. "Fu@#ing loser."

"Yeah. He's gonna be some lame psycho when he grows up. If we let him grow up."

"A lame psycho!" Joshua stated, chuckling as maniacally as ever. I felt tears start to well up in my eyes, and I didn't blink for fear of one falling down my cheek.

They both laughed like hyenas at me.

My teacher attempted to silence them, but the giggling and loudmouthed insults continued. They never listened to anyone.

I felt a tear meander down my cheek as they snickered. When the bell finally rang to exit the class, it was music to my ears, but it didn't help cheer me up. It was the old, "You can run, but you can't hide" thing for me. When I was a block away from school, I slowed up, noticing neither one of those jerks were following me. In all honesty, that did give me a lot of relief and it was good to get a full, deep breath once again. But I knew the relief was only temporary.

And, I also knew that I had been taking in all of their insults for far too long. It hurt long after I wasn't even within range of their voices. And I was embarrassed and ashamed of who I was, because I didn't even attempt to stand up for myself. I was completely broken mentally, and drained, physically.

When I was home, I greeted my mom and instantly went into my room. I laid down with my face buried in the pillow. I didn't cry or tear up, but I was overcome by an intense sadness. Somehow, even in all my leftover pain and with all of my ruminating, I fell asleep. When I woke up, it was 5:15 P.M. and I wanted to get a snack. I had two dollars on me, which I thought was enough to buy a candy bar from the nearby market. I got out of bed and headed out the door, into the living room. "Hey ma!" I called.

"What is it, Evan?" Mom answered.

"Is it okay if I go to the store real quick to get something?"

It took her a few seconds to respond. "That's fine. Just don't stay out there for too long, and wear a jacket! It's freezing out there!" She yelled back.

"Want me to get you anything?"

"I don't think so, Ev, but thanks for asking."

I walked into the kitchen, grabbed my black hoodie, and answered her "Okay, see you in a bit. Love you!"

I didn't hear her goodbye, but I thought nothing of it. And then, out the door I went, into the cold evening air.

After 5:00 PM, our street was always so quiet. And I walked down the lonely thoroughfare, being guided by the lamp poles that dotted the sidewalks. I shoved my bare hands into the pockets of my coat to protect myself from the bitter elements. The best part about going to the store, in my opinion, was the journey. I was alone with my thoughts, listening to music, and letting things go. It was quite relaxing. Something I needed desperately. Let me add, yes, relaxing, but only until I made it to the store.

Right outside the entrance, there were already shady-looking people. There was a man wearing a lavish coat smoking a cigar, which dangled from his mouth, and his arm was wrapped around a scantily clad woman with black streams of makeup rolling down her cheeks. I did my best to ignore the pair as I walked in.

The store was quiet, devoid of customers. It seemed like there was only me and a hawk-eyed clerk who kept his sights locked on me.

Seriously? Like I look like the criminal type after what I just saw outside the store!

I let the thought go and made my way toward the candy aisle. My eyes scanned over all the options, until the silence was broken by the sound of an all too familiar voice. Chills ran down my spine. I warily peered around the aisle and saw a group of five or six guys. And, in that crew, there they were – Joshua Robertson and Martin Cooper. Immediately I lost my appetite and decided to abandon the snack. I wandered around the candy shelf and then started speed walking toward the exit. From the corner of my eye, I caught a brief glimpse of Josh and Martin, who were making the same toothy smiles that I remembered from class. I picked up the pace, and ran out the door.

No way I'm hangin' around this place.

I got to the road and sprinted across it, ignoring the oncoming traffic. Frankly, I didn't care about getting hit by a car at that point, I just wanted to get back home. I was anxious anyway, so it was hard to breathe, and the running made it even worse. I started to move a little slower, but eventually I totally hyperventilated and I grinded to a complete halt. My heart jumped when I heard the sound of a familiar voice, "Goin' somewhere, freak?"

I quickly straightened myself back into an upright position and saw Joshua, Martin, and their group. "It's the lame kid." Martin pointed out.

Then, I heard one of the other guys crack his knuckles, another guy pounded on the corner newspaper box with his fists, while the rest of them talked over each other, every word an insult, a violation, a barb, in my direction. I gulped in fear and yet I didn't respond to what they were saying. "We wanna talk to you!" One kid yelled out. "Yeah, you need a good talkin' to!" another voice followed.

I tried to run. But, you know, like in a bad dream when you're fleeing a frightening situation, you think you're running but you're not getting anywhere, as if you're wearing cement shoes. That's what it was like for me. And I guess, looking back, it was because I was in a really bad state of shock. Suddenly, I felt a hand pull me by my shirt. It choked me. Then, I was pushed down onto the asphalt ground, under the glow of the streetlight, surrounded by darkness. "Nobody's here to help you. How's that feel? Ya scared?" Joshua threatened.

I tried hard to pull myself away from his grip, but when I did, I was kicked in the back by two other guys. I fell to the ground, got up again, and then this other kid, a BIG dude, came from behind me, punched my shoulder like he'd hit me with a brick, and it hurt like hell! It hurt so bad my left hand and fingers went numb for a moment.

I was surrounded. And I was scared. And with a few more knocks like that, I could also be tomorrow's local headline.

The whole group started beating me with powerful punches as I continued struggling to break free. Suddenly someone made a vicious uppercut and grazed my face with the large ring he was wearing. My nose was bleeding and a tooth fell out of my mouth — in pieces. One of the bullies pulled my Edgar Allan Poe book from my coat pocket and threw it into a nearby puddle. "We're doin' the world a favor! HIT 'IM HARDER!!!" another bully shouted.

I was running on fear, anxiety, and adrenaline. My legs felt like Jell-O. But even in the state I was in, I was remembering their faces. I needed to remember those faces! Then, I saw something from behind the group, emerging from the shadows of the night. It was another dark hooded figure. He was One Big Dude, and I knew that if he was coming after me, I might as well kiss my ass goodbye - permanently.

The pain of the blows stopped immediately.

Josh and Martin and their gang stepped back, as if they remembered this hooded character "WH-WHOA, DUDE!!! LISTEN, WAIT, HOLD ON, MAN!!! WE'RE COOL!!!"

The guys backed off and I could finally see what was going on. The hooded figure was wearing a leather jacket that was connected to what looked like a cape of some sort. I couldn't see his face because of the hood and shadows. Then, in a fast blur, he gave a left hook to one of my assailants, and sent him flying off the ground, landing the creep about six feet away from that first punch. I was in such shock I actually felt no pain. I stood there and watched this bully, writhing in agony, whimpering, and not *one* of his "best buddies" even moved an inch to help him.

To my imagination this stranger was reminiscent of Batman, with the cape and everything - if it was indeed a cape. He was obviously skilled in advanced martial arts. He was also obviously wise to the streets, and even more obviously, he appeared unknown to fear.

I stood there, wiping the blood away from my nose, my eyes, my mouth, and I lost not one but two teeth in the process. I watched in awe how this one man took each one of my attackers down to the ground, not one of them getting back up to continue the fight. The last two to fall were Martin and Joshua. And they had the purest look of fear in their eyes as this man fought with the ferociousness of a tiger. He flipped Josh and then Marty over into the bushes, effortlessly. I heard both of them moaning and crying. It was as if this man knew they were the main instigators. But how?

The other gang members started to get back up on their feet, not to fight - but to run away in fear. "I'm outta here! Screw this sh*t!" One of them yelled from a distance.

Eventually, Joshua and Martin were the only ones left. Still there watching fearfully from inside the brambles of two large bushes. "GET OUT HERE!" The hooded figure demanded. The sweat on their faces was glistening in the light as they raised their open hands, trembling. "We're cool. This ain't happenin' again, boss man. I swear to God." The figure looked over at me and then back at Josh and Martin. "Leave now or you'll never have another chance in this lifetime to do it!" The man boomed in a deep, foreboding voice.

With that, Joshua and Marty began walking slowly, backward, then eventually, turned to run away, at full speed and scared to death.

The hooded guy looked over at me. "You okay?" He calmly asked.

"Yes, sir. Th-thank you, so much, uh…" I praised, nervously. "Who are… I mean… how did you…"

I couldn't finish one single thought. He patted my shoulder. I noticed a smile beneath his hood. "Empower yourself, Evan. Band together with others for the good that's needed. I shouldn't have to exist."

He knows my name?

"Empower myself?! Do you *know* me? I can't do that. With what? I wouldn't even know where to start."

The man continued. "People like that, who attack your confidence are fully aware of your potential - even if you're not. I know what I'm talkin' about. I've been there. You can do this."

Then, the man disappeared into the night and I was left speechless.

As the mysterious vigilante fled into the darkness, I started walking home, ready to become a changed person. I thought deeply and carefully about what he said to me.

As I walked underneath the heavenly streetlights, I wiped away some blood that had dripped from my mouth. And I stood a bit taller as I heard his words again, "Fully aware of your potential - even if you are not. I've been there. You can do this." I began feeling a sense of pride, a feeling I was never accustomed to. Someone finally understood me.

This *hero* understood me.

An actual hero understood me.

I kept on walking, and thinking. And, with the knowledge that there was someone out there, someone operating in the night, protecting those who needed help most, it gave me even more hope. And that *hope* eventually turned into confidence. And I became proud of my differences and my self-esteem grew as I

176

became encouraged and inspired and invested in helping those who were in similar situations.

The Vigilante gave birth to a new me.

The old, insecure Evan would die, and in his place, in time, a new Evan would evolve into a crusader for all, someone who is: authentic, just, and honorable. It wouldn't happen overnight, but it would happen.

Many years after that fateful night, I decided to take it upon myself to don the mantle of the Vigilante and become a champion like that man, that crusader who saved me and altered the rest of my life.

And I learned, and I continue to learn that *all* people from all walks of life, can and do transform the world.

Their light shines everywhere.

Look for it.

"There are darknesses in life and there are lights,
and you are one of the lights, the light of all lights."

~Bram Stoker

Elijah Digirolamo is an eighteen-year-old senior at Piscataway High School. Elijah has always had passion for writing, spurred on by his fascination with horror movies and macabre-styled books.

He is an avid reader: fantasy, science-fiction, as well as superhero comic books. Elijah writes stories in many genres. He also enjoys drawing, watching movies, and hanging out with his friends. Elijah lives with his grandparents, Greg and Lisa Digirolamo, his younger brother, Scott, and his pet friends: Carly the dog, and Dusty and Cosmo- the cats.

Mr. Digirolamo is surely destined to become a famous fantasy, horror, or science-fiction author. Don't be surprised, if added into the mix, that he follows his dreams and also becomes a famous director/producer/screenwriter for the horror films of the future

"I know always that I am an outsider,
a stranger in this century and among those who are still men."

~H.P. Lovecraft

The Photographic Works
of
Jenna Stickel

"We don't see things as they are, we see them as we are."

~Anais Nin

Porch

The famous gingerbread houses in Martha's Vineyard are always seen as just beautiful houses. I wanted to get that extra element of the porch, because not many people look at the individual aspects of what makes these homes so stunning.

Niagara Falls

Niagara Falls at its most uncommon best. This particular shot was taken from directly 'Behind the Falls,' but, no matter what the angle, this natural wonder is the perfect photo opportunity for anyone with a camera.

Clemente Bridge

My love of Pittsburgh drew me to the gorgeous Roberto Clemente Bridge. With the history and beauty of this bridge practically screamed my name after a stormy day in Pittsburgh.

Cathedral

This magnificence of the St. Louis Cathedral in New Orleans practically found its own way into my camera. The building called to me so uniquely that I just couldn't possibly take a ordinary photograph.

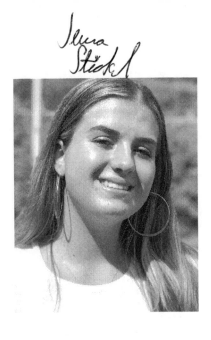

Jenna Stickel is a sixteen-year-old junior at Piscataway High School. Jenna proudly serves as secretary for Key Club, a world-wide volunteer organization, her appointment lasts for the duration of the 2018-2019 school year. She is also involved in the Fashion Club and participated in its fashion show at the end of her sophomore year. When Jenna finds the time she also busies herself with the school's newspaper, The Chieftain, and enjoys attending meetings for the Photography Club. On top of all that, she spends each winter watching basketball with her dad and his friends at Bound Brook High School. But, best of all, Jenna absolutely loves football! Her favorite team is the Pittsburgh Steelers. Jenna's dream is to one day move to Pittsburgh and work in sports management, while continuing her ever-growing love for photography.

"When there's nothing to believe in still you're coming back you're running back, you're coming back for more"

~The Eagles

The Written Works
of
Oriana Nelson

"A day without laughter is a day wasted."

~Charlie Chaplin

The Definition of Beauty

Beauty is a six-letter word that means a THOUSAND times more
than six letters.
Its ambiguity is clearly present, yet often overlooked,
Especially due to society's continuous efforts to define it for us,
As if we are incapable of doing so ourselves.

Society says that beauty is being skinny or "thick", but not fat.
Society says straight hair or curls are beautiful, but not afros.
Society says lighter complexions are better than darker ones.
Society says beauty is having a small nose, full lips and clear skin.

Well I am TIRED of what society says and its influence on *my*
perception of beauty.
No one should feel self-conscious because their characteristics
don't match typical beauty standards.
Self-love and confidence are essentials;
Don't allow society to make their achievement impossible!

You must define beauty on your own!

It may take years, or merely thirty minutes of reflection,

But no matter how long it takes, hopefully you'll discover someday,

A definition that makes *you* feel beautiful, inside and out

Meet Pessimism

Deep brown eyes overflowing
Like a submerged basin.
Face wet from the tears I cry for my future.
I'm scared.

Yet as I sit there and weep,
Bursts of laughter and shouts fill the room.
They *celebrate* while I *fear* for the worst.
Why am I scared while they're happy?

Maybe 'scared' doesn't fit the puzzle.
Maybe I'm just overwhelmed
By the millions of thoughts that
Race through my head.

Success, joy, and health,
May they be present in my future
Is a thought I *force* myself to think,
But deep down
I know that one minute
Won't make a difference.

Our brains are filled with fantasy.
These resolutions are annual
Broken promises to ourselves.
We never change
Like we plan to.

It's easy to fall into the trap-
To trick yourself into believing
That you'd finally change
After attempts every year.

But I don't fall anymore.
Instead I cry in fear
Of the year that lies ahead.
No need to get excited over false hopes.

Meet Optimism

The season of change
Has just arrived.
Time to start over
With a clean slate.

A cold wind blows
In all directions,
Forcing us to keep warm
With positive spirits.

We prance around
Excited for the new year.
Excited for another chance
To improve ourselves.

We are ready for
The rain showers of success,
The sunshine of happiness,
The spread of good health.

Show us what you
Have in store.
The year ahead
Must be bright!

Brighter than a star,
A shooting star that brings
To life all your new desires.

Every single one of them
Coming to life
Right before your very eyes.
This year will be my year.

All I Want For My Birthday

All the world's toys
Should be shared with
Other girls and boys.

I DO NOT need anymore,
They simply clutter the floor!
Trust me, I have enough on my own.
Excluding my siblings, I have over FIFTY alone!

So please don't give me toys this year
I do not think that I could bear.
I just want to do something fun,
Especially now that I'm six plus one!

Take me to the park
Or take me to the zoo
I'm sure I'll have fun
No matter what we do.

So no more toys and no more clothes.
I already have enough of those.
Just take me somewhere far or near.
I'm so excited my birthday is finally here!

Worry

I worry that one day
His body would lay
Helplessly inside of a university.
Whatever happened to the promise of security?

Tall, black, unafraid to speak their mind,
Perfectly describes the victim every time.
My dad, my cousin, my brother
I could easily lose one or the other.

The fear that his name would appear on a news headline
Engulfs me and I lose my mind.
And I tremble and tremble
As his final words in my brain assemble:
"Please don't shoot, I'm…"

But I close my eyes,
Permanently erasing this horrid state of mind
That my body has grown accustom to.
It is time for the death of the roots
That allow such growth.
And it is time to make a change.

Today I call for the extinction

Of school shootings,

And an end to acts of terrorism.

Today is the last day

Bullets can pierce the skin

Of a colored being without validity.

Our laws need revision.

And we must revise them

As if we are the greatest editors

Of all time.

We all possess the gift of speech.

It's called a gift for a reason.

Let it be heard,

Let it improve the laws that curse our land.

These gun laws need to be amended.

I don't deserve all this worry.

You don't either.

Nobody does.

Chandelier

The chandelier in this Toronto hotel lobby was absolutely gorgeous. Through the adjustment of the focus lens, I was able to create a bokeh effect that I was ecstatic about! It was my first time successfully practicing bokeh photography,

Bokeh: The blur out-of-focus objects within a photograph.

Oriana Nelson is a seventeen-year-old honor roll student attending her junior year at Piscataway High School. She has a strong passion for: dancing, singing, and photography. One day she hopes her photographs will be featured in a museum or in a prominent, worldwide magazine.

Oriana also has interests unrelated to art such as: spending quality time with her parents, Betty-Anne and Curtis, along with her three siblings, Oona, Curtis, and Olesia. As a family they often bike ride together which is one of Oriana's favorite outdoor activities. During the school year, she focuses more on extracurricular activities such as: marching band and multiple academic clubs. Through these clubs Oriana has learned many a valuable skill such as: the importance of public speaking, time management, and working well with others.

"Desire is the key to motivation, but it's the determination and commitment to unrelenting pursuit of your goal - a commitment to excellence - that will enable you to attain the success you seek."

~Mario Andretti

The Written Works
of
Yumna Enver

"Lightning makes no sound until it strikes."

~Martin Luther King Jr.

Reckoning

Time had swathed the laboratory in streaks of spider silk, gossamer threads floating between ripples of deep ocean. The cables snake between tools of decayed metal, leaving gentle valleys through dust coated floors; a harmony reached only from centuries of existence sown in past recollection. The sole source of light was the lines of green code, dripping down towers of stacked screens. A halo of incomprehensible chitter, divine gospel to the man perched in front of them, fingers ghosting over the keys in a possessed fervor. Code bled from the veins lining the underside of translucent skin, stretched precariously over protruding knuckles and wound tightly down attenuated fingers. Dark, ribbon strands brush past caved cheeks and slink down a faded lab-coat draped shoulder. Time pauses her decoration, sitting back with keen eyes and decides that perhaps mischief longs another waltz with the tortured scientist.

It is a faint tapping that skims the very edge of comprehension that makes Kanae still, thoughts unhindered by coherent reason surfacing--a cork bobbing in and out of unending sea. Fatigue slides easy hands across his shoulders, dropping weights on Kanae's fluttering eyelids and yet, the noise persists--a stuttering heart cannot be ignored. The chair whines as he shifts slowly toward the sound, eyes suddenly wide as the stench of burning flesh, something floral, and a faint temperature rise drifts jellyfish teacups around his being. They smell of the days that slipped past reaching fingers and causes Time to giggle behind a finger pressed lip. Joints crack as he moves to stand, groaning quietly when his knees buckle beneath him. He takes in a rasping breath and rises, scanning the oblivion that extends before him. His eyes fall to the glass cell in the far corner of the laboratory, fogged and illuminated ever so slightly. He shuffles toward the cell, arms outstretched, as if his memory would betray him just this once. The noise, louder now and insistent, drum shivers down a knobbed spine.

Time lays a blanket of hush in his path, humming all the while. The glass whines, and then there is an emergence of limbs, dark and ichor streaked.

The figure falls limp from the broken cell, shivering. Kanae swallows thickly and pushes forward, uneasy and yet emboldened, gripped by a blooming curiosity. When he is close enough to hear a faint sobbing he reaches out, fingers just shy of making contact. Exhaling heavily, apprehension curled fingers unfurl as he gingerly strokes the damp, silver shaven strands. His hands slip down, tracing the shimmering lines that slink down the creature's skin in patterns of disarray. Otherworldly, it leaves Kanae entranced and unaware of the floor, wine-pooled and tipsy. A tremor grips the figure and wind chimes coo from a heart melted and remolded.

Tendrils rip from the figure in shards of reflecting obsidian, glinting, formidable--blurred? Seconds split into fractions, Kanae stares at the pointed fingers with mild surprise, wrapped loosely around his neck. The screens behind him shriek to the tune of Time's clock--hand turned baton, dimly illuminating the oddities of the creature's face.

"Oh," Kanae breathes, hands coming to cradle the face hovering before him.

"Hello, darling." He whispers, mouth quirking when her head tilts in confusion. He wets his lips and smiles pleasantly.

"It really has been quite a while; don't you think? I have *so* much to tell you, my dear." He rasps, tears pooling the corners of shadow-bled eyes.

She does not respond, save for the slight turning down of her lips. They are still, God and Creation. (Except this man is not God and this creature is not his wife, whom he so dearly loved). Kanae leans in closer, the cartilage of his neck straining tenderly against her hold. His features twisted into something vile, pulled wide with threads of insanity. His gaze flits erratically between her blank stare--feeling his ribs collapsing on a heart that no longer wishes for a past love, a skull caving into a brain that no longer delights in wistful musings.

"Do you even know who you are? Do you know...who *I* am?" he sneers, letters torn from a metal embedded throat. The figure continues to stare silently, eyes round and impossibly bright.

"No," they finally rasp, blinking just once. Their hold on Kanae's neck slackens. The spikes protruding from their back melt, drips down to snake their body in inky lines, shimmering against the undulating lights.

"I do not."

The figure moves to stand, sluggish but sure in its movements. Their head, limp between their shoulders lift, chin raised, with a cheek pressed to a shoulder, gazing down at Kanae. They reek of vanity, regality spilling down their shoulders in jewel laden furs, soft and glimmering. If he squints, he can see the furs soaking up the spilled alcohol, staining it a muted rose. Under this new gaze, Kanae forgets himself, overcome with a firm desire to do nothing but gape, for this figure of unholy divinity was—was—

"I do not know of your beloved or of yourself," The figure's eyes flutter shut, reveling in something Kanae cannot perceive.

"I only know of myself." Kanae now peers curiously at the figure, eyelids tripping on Fatigue's stretched legs and into Slumber's open arms. The alcohol churns and floats in quaint pastel bubbles.

"Who are you, then?" The words are heavy, slurred between parted lips. His world is stained berry, details losing their edges, the pull of long denied rest dragging him into unconsciousness. The figure kneels, grasping his jaw and pulls him forward. Kanae stumbles and yet, he finds himself leaning into the figure's warmth.

The figure grins, sugar spilling past cherry blossom lips and trickling onto the floor in large pools of saccharine malice.

"Why, Kanae..." The figure murmurs,

Kanae's eyes fall shut, the jaw beginning to part before him not entirely unwelcome. Time holds her breath, silk spun skirts clutched in eager anticipation.

"What else can I be but your reckoning?"

[carrying marble busts as mirrors,
i have drowned in velvet waters]

tell me the secret of writing pretty words for i cannot find myself
creating beauty what does one expect, crafting with fingers
blueberry kissed? at times i dream in fine silks and piled velvets
but mostly i do not dream of such things, just a warm hand to
hold that i really just wish was my own. i wish for my life to be
penned by authors that like to see the world drowned peach and
adorned with the finest of golds, where even monotony is
glorified. is it the music that strings midnight threads between
the corners of my eyes or are they merely being pulled from a
heart that beats simmering blood and courses under flesh that
does not feel like my own, oh, why must i think of cherry picked
lips and glass skin? why must i seek this out in souls that i do not
intend to treat with the secrets that unhinge my ribs and unravel
my flesh into languid caramel. i am so very in love with you i
love the way you love me, like a fool blindly wrapping ripped
cloth over eyes that knows but still wishes to not embrace action
because the world looks quite the thing drowned in gauzy
oceanic hues. i wonder what my bones will be sculpted in before
they splinter and i wonder what my blood will become, frothy
and lively as it churns before it settles and flows only for
another. or perhaps my blood will remain as it is, slipping down
veins that will always whisper of what it will be until my mind
skims pretty lines down my face and whispers that i will never
be what it should have been despondency has my jaw locked in a
firm grasp and intense cerulean fires caress the ember charred
bones lining my velvet flesh, embedded in them like fine
weaponry and the other fine things my being will never behold. i
only ask to be drawn in soft lead and immortalized in blurred
whispers.

[holy ramblings]

time skims tongues in the shape of flower petals,
shaping ones predicament into one that does not feel like it will
last

there is sun and you have been claimed for it is just from the
corner of my eye where apollo aims with citrus spun arrows and
my, they have never looked so sweet

things are strange, strange, strange to a heart unfurled, ribs
unhinged, voraciously insatiate

flower-petal time tastes bitter on a tongue that lulls omen hymns,
the warmth seeps quickly out of things not woven from flesh,

apollos nectar-dipped arrows have gone cold for i found sadness
only after i licked them clean.

[eloquence tends to falter
when she sees your face]

i haven't been the same since your lips bloomed against my skin-
-bloomed and wilted, whispers of strawberry jam and drowsy
angel wings--with keys hanging from your hips you traverse my
ribs, wrapping every sharp crevice with velvet ribbons, stringing
cherry pits as you slip through every marshmallow step i have
left for you--and as you dance through my being i find myself in
yours, lace, tulle, and cotton clouds, my fallen peach seeds
lulling themselves in the spaces between your mural-painted
bones (i thought flowers would look quite pretty) at night i sleep
soundly in the center of your heart murmuring letters (only you
can hear them) and perhaps, perhaps, perhaps i love you is all too
cliché (it is) but (you said) there is a reason clichés are clichés so
maybe ten million i love you's is ten million ways of me trying
to tell you that i think you are the best thing that has happened to
my heart--rosé drunk letters have never fallen from my carnation
lips and yet when you're around (you make me feel so cozy)
gold (home is where you are) accents (home is where you want
to be) my (wherever you are) tongue (you can come home to me)

Yumna Enver was born and raised in Piscataway, New Jersey. She is currently a Junior at Piscataway High School and is looking forward to her final year as a Senior. She has always loved to express herself creatively, whether it be through writing or art. She enjoys creating poetry and short stories. She comes from a family of six: hardworking and loving parents, two older sisters and one brother. Though undecided, she hopes she can apply her writing skills to any field she chooses to study. In her free time, she enjoys drawing, listening to music, watching shows and spending time with Julia, her best friend and longtime partner in crime.

"It is never too late to be what you might have been."

~George Eliot

The Written Works
of
Ameerat Bisiolu

"I know that I am intelligent,
because I know that I know nothing."

~Socrates

<u>Alone</u>

Every Saturday was colder than the one before. No matter the day, week, season, or year, the day always looked the same to me. Dark clouds heavy with precipitation. Wind laced with spiteful icicles. The illusion of a storm, one ready to knock out the world, followed me everywhere… on Saturdays.

Today, the sky was particularly uneasy. I walk on waterlogged feet holding a dozen crimson red roses. They barely weighed a pound, yet they somehow carried the weight of the world. I was shackled to them, my fingers clutching the various stems as if they would somehow save me, or pull me out of my commitment.

But that's exactly what this is — a commitment. I'd been putting off this obligation for far too long, and there was no better time than today.

The first drop of rain trickled down my forehead, a cool contrast against my burning skin. I was so wrapped up in the world: the way the wind rose and fell in volume, the swaying of the graveyard cypresses, the fluttering of birds' wings as they flew south. I crouched in the grass, feeling the thin blades slice into my bare knees. My eyes fell to the ground; I couldn't bring myself to look up. Instead, I lifted my hand and ran it against the dull gray rock. Grass and vegetation crept over the edges of the headstone, almost obscuring the name that I'd never forget.

"Hi, Charlie," I said to the grave. I trace the indentations on the stone, feeling every one of them until I knew what it spelled: *November 28, 2002 - December 17, 2018.*

"I feel like I shouldn't be here," I started, the words coming out rushed. "It's been so long, I thought that maybe you'd be better off if I left you alone. Maybe you *prefer* being far from here. So you can be the only version of you that exists."

I was scrambling for something to say to justify my absence. But nothing could explain four years of us being apart. Nothing could explain me spending my seventeenth, eighteenth, and nineteenth birthdays without my sister.

"I was really angry," I remember. I was sitting on the couch between my parents the day the police told us. "You were always so confident and happy. Everything was going so right…"

I wish she would reply. Like always, she gave me the silent treatment. The wind died, and the leaves stopped swaying. Some of the birds were gone.

"But that was the problem, right? Everything was going so right, so perfect. It was perfect because you were with him. Your mystery guy. The guy that you knew you shouldn't have been with. That's why you kept him a secret. Because you knew that any sensible adult would have called the police on him."

I dig my fingers into the side of the grave. The sharp rock cuts into the palm of my hand.

"The worst part is that I knew something was off. I knew it wasn't right, the way you kept him completely off my radar. You loved to overshare, especially with me. Classic little sister things. You'd always look for my approval - even when you said you didn't care about it."

I had a memory of my sister, her face identical to mine yet not as sad. She was more angelic and approachable than I could ever hope to be. I imagined her scowling at my usage of the words *little sister*. Her bow-shaped lips would twist into a sneer, irritation building in those pea-green eyes we shared. She'd hit me and say, *"A few minutes don't mean a thing."*

The cypress she is buried under sways gently. The wind comes back. A confused bird flies in circles, honking to its clan. Another drop of rain falls, then another, both landing on Charlie's grave. They leave dark teardrop stains against the rock, identical to the tears I shed.

Another memory of my sister, a happier one, spreads a smile on my face. I tuck my hair behind my ear and wipe my runny nose with the hem of my t-shirt. "I remember when we were younger, like five or six, and you begged mom to let you get a haircut. She kept telling you no. So you woke me up at 1:00 a.m., had me hold a mirror and a flashlight in front of you, and chopped half of your hair off. You hated it, but liked the look of horror on mom's face. Her reaction was reward enough for you.

"And what about that time we met Prince Charming at Disneyland when we were thirteen? He was smoking a cigarette behind a bathroom building. We ran away from Mom and Dad and just saw him standing there, wondering if it was a good time to ask for his autograph. I wanted to stand back, but you were so confident." I chuckle at the thought of Charlie's determination, her words, *"Come on April, let's go!"* ringing in my head.

"And you always had the biggest crushes," I say. "You'd talk to a guy for a second, and then have your lives together outlined in thirty seconds. It's crazy that I'm the one who ended up with a boyfriend first. That made you so mad."

A steady rain falls. The tree bends its back in woe. The circling bird is gone, its distant laughter echoing in the silent evening. The wind blows the flowers out of my arms, spreading their colorful seeds across the cemetery. I wrap my hands around my bare knees.

"I guess that's why you went to him, isn't it? You thought that if I could get a boyfriend so quickly and you couldn't, something was wrong with you. So you ran to Dorian and thought that an older guy would make you feel better about yourself."

Icy rain. Violent swaying of the tree. A chorus of birds exits the scene. Lightning briefly turns night to day, and thunder quickly follows, shaking the ground with the fury of a thousand storms. Yet Charlie is silent, letting the world do the talking for her.

"You were so insecure, you ran to this psychopath and fell in love with him. You loved him up until he stuck a knife through your heart."

I lean over the grave, no longer afraid of looking at the wet stone. *Charlie Spaulding: November 28, 2002 - December 17, 2018. Perky spirit, loving sister, and unforgettable daughter.*

"Sometimes I wish I could forget you," I hiss. "But I can't, or else I'll be alone. And I can't live like that. I'm... scared. I've never been on my own."

The sky cries with me, dumping a bucket of sorrow into my open palms. I hear the moan of the wind as it wraps me in a chilly hug, whistling a fateful tune into my ear. *I'm still here. I'll never leave you.*

"How could you leave me on my own?"

I clutch at the grave and let out choppy breaths, gulping for air that would never come.

"How could you..."

But Charlie stays silent as the world rages on, giving me all the answers I need, and yet nothing at all.

206

Hollow

In the hallways of our home
Without the pitter-patter of your feet
I have to stop and think;

Where did you go?
Are you eating?
Are you sleeping?
Do you miss us?
Do you miss
Me?

It is something that cannot be said over the phone.
I miss you, in all your irritations and annoyances.
I miss the sound of weekend cartoons
And your loud, boisterous laugh.

Not dead and gone,
But your identity is buried.
For I, and only I, will see
How they destroyed you.
And the little boy I knew will come back
An indifferent man.

But until that day
I will hold your memory fondly in my heart,
and sit and pray.
Pray that when you're back
This home will not be so hollow.

Ameerat Bisiolu is a junior at Piscataway High School. She has always had an affinity for the arts, specifically for writing.

Ameerat enjoys writing at every given opportunity: on the bus, in the car, and even before she goes to bed. She is the fourth in a line of five children, preceded by two older brothers, Faruq and Sulaiman, an older sister, Munirah, and is followed by her youngest brother, Imran. Their parents, Omololu and Sekinat, support them all. Ameerat discovered her passion for writing in the fourth grade. Since then she has been dreaming of becoming an author. Aside from making her passion her future career, Ameerat has also found love in psychology and hopes to become a clinical psychologist. Outside of that, Ameerat enjoys listening to music, reading, and teaching children at her Masjid on the weekend.

"And by the way, everything in life is writable about if you have the outgoing guts to do it, and the imagination to improvise. The worst enemy to creativity is self-doubt."

~Sylvia Plath

The Written Works
of
Dorothy Seaboldt

"Don't just teach your children to read...teach them to question what they read. Teach them to question everything."

~George Carlin

Please Do Not Erase

(The Heartbreaking Saga of No.2)

I stand tall.

At attention.

My mind is sharp. At the peak of its intellect.

Everything about me. Untouched. Unused.

Brand new.

Yet upon that first day, everything changed,

As I waltzed into battle,

You picked me up.

You threw me down, Fastened your grip tighter.

I hit the surface **hard.**

You hung me upside down.

My mind being drained. My insides being dragged around,
Just to cause me pain.

Then... You let me go.

You let me down.

I hit the cold ground.

My mind now dull and broken.

My heart now shattered to bits.

Then... I'm picked up.

Being taken away to an unknown place.

Just to be tortured again.

The unknown place: A dark hole with Spinning blades.

I was forced in, I was spun around. **Slowly getting wound down.** My mind gets sharper, **Just to benefit you**.

Therefore I lose my battle.

I somehow believe I'm safe from this, That the war is well and done.

I **should** feel at peace.

I am then locked away for days and days, Hearing not a single sound. That was until that fateful day, When I heard the news,

And saw that I had been used.

So please do not erase the work that I have done,

Because I know that it was my brain, that got **your job done.**

Scars

Acne since she was in 3rd grade. The scars that have been left behind crowding up her face. So she covers up her scars. Scared of how she looks. Burdened by what others say. Her make up covers her scars, as she hopes that they will fade.

Little does she know *she's beautiful* **even with those scars.**

Another girl, Broken down by the world. Torn apart by her family. Ashamed to be herself. Scared to wear shorts because of the scars on her legs. Scared to talk to her family and telling them she is gay. She cuts them up more and more everyday.

Little does she know *she's loved* by her friends **even with those scars.**

Finally a little boy, born with a pain that he could not erase. Surgery at only a couple months old, His parents were praying for grace. He has to grow up with a scar over his heart Unable to do things that all the other kids can do.

He's beaten, broken, and bullied too. Little does he know, *his bullies* **are broken too.**

We **all** have scars. We've **all** been hurt. Inside we're **all** the same. We're **all** broken down. We've **all** been thrown around.

And here's my last thing to say...

Embrace those scars. *Embrace* those stories. Don't be afraid let them to show. Because those scars made you who you are.

And it's time to let them know.

The Story of a Distressed Author

There is an author,

Somewhere in this world. An author
without a thought.

A person on this earth, Who is good
with words, Yet not.

They will sit for days, Just
waiting. Waiting on that thought.

And one day it will appear. It will
appear, But will be forced to rot.

There is an author,

Somewhere in this world. An author with
no voice.

Their voice is unheard. Unheard,But not
by choice.

Their words, Tend to escape them. But
not by their own design.

They honor their words, Praying for a
day,

When they can openly shine

There is an author,

Somewhere in this world. An author
writing *this* down.

An author with a voice. A voice that
screams, So it can be heard all around.

An author with the choice. To make
choices, That *should* be made.

An author with the courage. The courage to speak for the ones, Whose words are often swayed.

There is an author,

Somewhere in this world, Who speaks for those who can't.

Who takes the words, That have been stolen, And allows their seeds to plant.

They stand for those, Without the freedom.

The freedom to speak their own words.

The author on this earth

Frees those words from their captives...

In order to conquer worlds.

Dorothy Seaboldt is a sixteen-year-old 10th grade student at Piscataway High School. In her free time she enjoys reading novels and short stories by authors such as: Ray Bradbury, Ransom Riggs, and Stephen King. Dorothy likes to write stories in the historical fiction, horror, and mystery genres *along with the poetry presented in this book*. During the school year Dorothy volunteers with the Piscataway High School Air Force Junior ROTC and 'P-Way Buddy Ball' which is a program in Piscataway where students play sports and games with disabled children of all ages. Dorothy loves spending time with her mother and father; Angela and George and going shopping, to the movies, and out to eat with her friends: Justin, Emily, and Maritza. Dorothy's plans for the future are: to go to college, get a doctorate in psychology, and to help children in need from all backgrounds, races, and nationalities.

Dorothy Seaboldt

"Our greatest weakness lies in giving up. The most certain way to succeed is always to try just one more time."

~Thomas A. Edison

The Written Works
of
Semira Lewis

"Fear is the mind killer."

~Frank Herbert

Feeling

I wake up.
I didn't know I was asleep.
I didn't know I was ALIVE in the first place.
I don't know who I am or where I am.
I don't what I am.
But I can feel and see and think…
Apparently?
Is that what it's called?
"Thinking."
I try to push myself up with these limbs I have.
They touch multiple cold, wet, and soft strands.
I look at what I am touching.
These strands give off a very bright and vibrant color.
- PROCESSING -
…
…..
……..
Grass.
That's what it's called!
I guess I'm
- PROCESSING -
…
…..
……..
Outside.
Huh…? That's a very bright, and vibrant light source.
It's seems to be radiating heat to me and everything
surrounding me. It's the
- PROCESSING -
…
…..
……….

Sun. I start to notice where I am. Multiple...
- PROCESSING -

...

.....

....

Trees surround me. But I sense I'm not alone. Something rumbles in the distance, different pitches of sound.
I turn toward the direction I heard it from.
I notice other lifeforms huddled within a group.
They let out the variety of sounds
Filled with
- PROCESSING -

...

.....

....

Joy?
I hide behind a shorter tree.
What are those sounds? Is it...
- PROCESSING -

...

.....

....

Laughter?
Is that what it's called?
I wonder why they do that?
Listening to them laugh makes me laugh. It's contagious.
HAHAHA
It fills me with so called "JOY." Suddenly something red flashes in front of me.
-WARNING! WARNING! **OVERHEATING!**-
I stop laughing and stay in the shade.
I artificially breathe in.
And out.
I start cooling off when I hear another sound.
I face that direction.
It's kind of an annoying sound.
Though I feel...?

218

- PROCESSING -

...

.....

....

Miserable?
It's
- PROCESSING -

...

......

....

Wailing. A smaller version of the earlier life forms is
"wailing".
It seems to have lost their balloon.
I suddenly filled with dread and filled with
Sorrow.
I start to cry.
I'm not sure why. Yet again red flashes in front of me.
-WARNING! WARNING! **OVERHEATING!**-
I stop crying and stay in the shade.
I artificially breathe in.
And out.
I start cooling off when I hear another sound.
This time it's loud. It makes my hearing sensors ring.
- PROCESSING -

...

......

....

Yelling, screaming, shouting.
I look over and see people push someone around.
- PROCESSING -

...

....

....

Taunting them.
Something about it makes me want to
Scream

Shout
I want them to
STOP.

I think this is
- PROCESSING -
...
....
....
Anger.

I start to get out of the shadows.
Into the sun's rays.
I walk toward them.
I starting heating up. The red flashing starts again but I
Ignore it.
-WARNING! WARNING! **OVERHEATING!**-
I start seeing a different kind of red
-WARNING! WARNING! **OVERHEATING!**-
I'm shaking.
I'm shaking with
RAGE
I am about to reach them.
I am about to show them my...
Anger.
I start violently shaking.
My anger controls me.

I stop for a brief second.
I try to calm down but
I just realize that this whole time
I've been
- PROCESSING -
...
.....
......

Fe...eling? I recollect my memories of feeling in this short time.
I didn't think that was possible. I felt warmth, joy, sorrow, and now rage.
I try to wrap my head around it
But it's not making any sense.
It's overwhelming
I'm overheating
I shouldn't
Be able
To
Feel
I'm-

I'm-

A-

-WARNING! WARNING! UNSTABLE CONDITIONS!
YOU WILL SELF DESTRUCT IN **3... 2... 1-**

Anxiety

I breathe in
I breathe out
I shake out all the doubt

I look up
I stand out

I don't think ``what about''

My Song...

I want to sing out
I want to be heard
Just like all the other birds

They sing their songs
Sing about anything they want
And they get attention and so, they flaunt

Whether it's good or bad
They are now known
But now I feel oh, so alone

Sing out says everyone<u>!</u>
Let them <u>know</u>
the **lyrics** in your *soul*

It's not that I don't want to
It's not that I can't
It's that I fear to start singing a useless rant

Yet I want to sing out
Yet I want to be heard
Just like all the other birds.

Semira Lewis is a fifteen-year-old sophomore at Piscataway High School. She's always liked drawing and writing.

The passions she has include drawing, writing, and making music. The musical instruments she plays are the double bass and the soprano ukulele. Music is played for the pure enjoyment and continuation of music in her family. Her family is quite large and she holds everyone close to her heart.

"You don't have to teach people how to be human. You have to teach them to stop being inhuman."

~Eldridge Cleaver.

The Written Works
of
Kainat Azhar

"In a gentle way, you can shake the world."

~Mahatma Gandhi

Unfathomable

What is it that bothers me?
For sometimes the pain becomes so unbearable
That I am left speechless
With nonexistent tears
Streaming silently down my face
Every single teardrop
Holding the weight of the ocean
I am left baffled
Tearing myself apart in frustration
Because I do not understand
Why I can be content
But not happy
Yet at the same time
Be happy
Yet not content
Incomplete and unsatisfied
What is it that
Contorts my vision
Of the world
And leaves me feeling
Like I am a spectator
As if I am standing behind the lenses
On the camera of life
Feeling awfully disconnected
From everyone around me
Why is it that
The entire world
Seems to surround me
Suffocate me
Press its fingers

Onto the windows of my heart
Like a child
Eyeing a red velvet cake
In the glass window
Of a prestigious shop
Yet unlike the cake
Beautiful and inviting
I am left confused
Shocked and rattled
Pushing the palms of my hands
Onto my overwhelmed ears
To block out a sound
That isn't even there

Beauty

How dare you
How dare you tell us
That we are not good enough
Unless society appreciates our adornments
As if our sole purpose in life
Is to flaunt our assets
As if all we've got
Is only what you see
How dare you demean us
As if we have nothing more to offer
Than our porcelain doll faces
How dare you
Label us as weak and vulnerable
As if we are crying out for help
Begging to be saved

Why don't you
Remove the blindfold
That is suffocating you
And open your eyes
Why don't you
Clear that wax out of your ears
So that you can better hear
How little you know about us
Let me prove to you
How capable we are

Today
I'm going to show you
That words like "pretty" and "delicate"
Were not made to lure us in

Or define us
I'm going to show you that beauty
Does not necessarily lie in
A perfectly sculpted face and body
No, darling
Beauty lies in the raw skin
It lives in the bones
Its home is the heart
It's pure and innocent
And how will you ever be able to see true beauty
If your eyes aren't even open?

Let me tell you that my face
Does not equate what I'm worth
Your accusations and scornful remarks
Are going to become my footstool
To stand up tall, proud, and strong
So that you recognize
How awfully mistaken you are
Because that is what beauty is
It doesn't hide; it doesn't run
It stays put and defies the world

Remember Me

We are the generation of people
Who want to overachieve
We want that label of appreciation
We want to be admired

For what?
For the straight A's we aspire for
Spending nights poring over texts
Without really understanding the content?

For the ones we push below us
To stand proudly on their piles of bones?
For pointing out the skeletons in their closets
While we've got houses full of our own?

No
We want to be remembered
Merely to be remembered
So that they can glorify us

We *live* for our names to be proudly announced
To a world that could care less
We want to maintain false images of ourselves
To appease others

We want to boast about the triumphs
We've never faced
We want to strive for notorious labels
Without really living up to them

We want to work, work, work
Without acknowledging the dark circles beneath our eyes

The sleep deprivation
The dead weight on our shoulders

We just want that "Wow!" to be whispered about us
So that they know what great things we've done
Even if we cry ourselves to sleep at night
For the lies we've told, the people we've wronged

When will we realize
That the world is but a jury?
And what are we
But cases to be examined?

When will we finally realize
That in their eyes
No matter how much we stumble and strive
We will never win?

But
It doesn't matter, right?
As long as they are aware of
The sleepless nights I've wasted

I am content
So long as they have heard of me
So long as they
Remember me

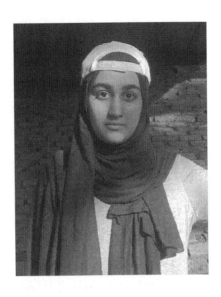

Kainat Azhar is a sixteen-year-old girl who attends Piscataway High School. She is a slightly funny person and loves making others laugh. She enjoys reading and writing—especially poetry—and for as long as she can remember, becoming an author has been her very first dream. In the future, Kainat would like to become a mental health therapist because she finds peace in helping others. As a side job/hobby, she would like to continue writing books and poetry for her own pleasure.

"Your work is going to fill a large part of your life, and the only way to be truly satisfied is to do what you believe is great work. And the only way to do great work is to love what you do. If you haven't found it yet, keep looking. Don't settle. As with all matters of the heart, you'll know when you find it."

~Steve Jobs

PISCATAWAY HIGH SCHOOL WRITERS GUILD

Many thanks from The Teen Writers Guild to:

The Piscataway School Board:
We will be eternally grateful to all of you for having the heart and the wisdom to know the lifelong magic and majesty that this Writers Guild has given to each and every one of us. We are forever changed.

Dr. Frank Ranelli:
Your perfectly timed phone call to Judith Kristen made this empowering, learning, and magnificent ride possible.
Because of that connection we have learned that effectiveness, proper communication, along with deep understanding and respect for ourselves and others is paramount to a fulfilled personal and professional life. You are the best!

Mr. Robert Coleman:
Thank you for starting the Guild Ball rolling, - welcoming the possibility and helping to facilitate our beginnings. We enjoyed seeing you check-in during summer sessions at our local library, and during the school year at our own PHS library as well. You even thought of us for the PiscatawayREADS Celebration, giving a few of our guild writers, the chance to speak about the difference the guild has made in our lives. Thank you for everything.

Cathline Tanis:
We thank Mrs. Tanis for understanding us, and the importance of this experience at this time in our lives. Also for: scheduling our assemblies, creating and distributing flyers and invitations, and making sure we had our much needed 'in school' library time with Ms. Kristen as well. Also a huge thank you for putting together our beautiful Celebration Event – making it a part of our lives we will never, ever forget!

Frank Sinatra:
The time you spent with us in school and at our local library was enlightening, informative, and valuable to our art in more ways than we could ever express. And, our "Left of Center" cover that

you designed was even more than we hoped it would be. It spoke for us as well as for our work before a page was even turned.

Ronni Garret:
A Guild Member herself, Ronni helped Frank Sinatra interview fellow guild members and took biography photos as well. She gave of herself not only as an author, she gave of herself as a well-represented part of Piscataway High School media. Her star will always shine brightly. It can be no other way.

Zach Martin:
Zach shows his art in the form of photographs. One spoke so loud and clear it was unanimously decided that it would be used as the back cover art for the Guild book. It is certain to remain a classic for decades to come.

PHS Librarian, Kathleen Memoli:
We thank you for opening your heart and your library to us. Thank you for your supportive words of ecouragement, your interest in our creations, and your understanding of just how much this project meant to all of us. You are an amazing woman!

JFK Library, Piscataway, New Jersey:
Located on Hoes Lane just blocks from Piscataway High School, this beautiful little library and its lovely librarians welcomed us week after week for hours on end to complete our collective works. We all look forward to the day we find our book within the shelf space of this most cherished and respected building.
We thank you from the bottom of our hearts.

Judith Kristen:
The woman who brought this book together, Judith Kristen tirelessly and wholeheartedly worked to make our dreams a reality. Thank you for the time and grit you put into our work. Every moment with you has been enlightening, fun, and thoroughly enjoyable.
We love you and we're grateful to you far beyond what words could ever say.

AND IN THE END...

From Judith Kristen:

In May of 2018, at the request of Dr. Frank Ranelli, I spoke to four Piscataway High School assemblies to recruit hopefuls for this book. One hundred and sixty-two students wrote to me and eagerly stated that they wanted to be a part of this first-ever Teen Writers Guild at their school

And, during the summer of 2018 those numbers dropped for many a legitimate reason:

"I really don't have the time to give."

"I'd like to, but I play sports."

"It's more work than I thought it would be."

"I have a job."

"I have to babysit."

So, within three months, the numbers went from one hundred and sixty-two hopefuls to twenty-six of Piscataway's most tenacious.

Their eye was on the journey as well as the end result. And they were going to see it through from start to finish.

Straight off I made it clear that this was **not** a school project. This was an accountable life lesson that was not designed to fade away any time soon.

By the time you get to read this, everything is already a beautiful done deal.

The book is in your hands, the Guild members writing, re-writing, and editing, editing, editing, is complete, the celebration party is over, first time authors have autographed hundreds of books by now, and they are all moving forward with this amazing new knowledge, embracing the friendships they've made, and beaming with pride and joy over their first published work - as they should be.

But, for me, right now as you're reading this, I'm still in the process of putting their work in its proper place and position, re-reading one last time all of the work they have completed. And, as I see each and every one of their photographs placed above their biographies, I recall more than their faces. I hear the excitement in

238

their voices, "My writing is *actually* going to be in a book! MY writing! MY Photos! MY Art!"

I also hear the grumbles that came with the words, "What?! Another Edit?!!"

And, I see their smiles and hear their laughter, and recall the pride on those faces because they knew they had measured up to the task.

This was a demanding piece of work.

It meant deadlines, rewrites, and giving up their Saturdays to meet with me at the JFK Library time after time over their summer vacation. It meant over 2,000 emails in total and dozens upon dozens of phone calls between us – to get it right.

And they did.

They came to me as: freshmen, sophomores, juniors, and seniors.

They left me as: artists, authors, and friends – with a genuine, unwavering, and high-spirited fire in their furnace.

To say I am proud of these Guild members would be a huge understatement.

I am honored and blessed to know each and every one of them. I have enjoyed all of the time I spent with these wonderful artists.

And, I have great hope for their futures because I have seen with my own eyes, what they can do when they put their heart, mind, and soul into something.

...Let the magic continue.

Judith Kristen
March 21, 2019

"A hundred years from now it will not matter what my bank account was, the sort of house I lived in, or the kind of car I drove... but the world may be different because I was important in the life of a child."

~Forest Witcraft

If you can read this, thank a teacher.

For Nicole....
You have the
heart of a poet
and the courage
of a Lion!!
It will take you
far!! — Peace & Love
Judy

Judith Kristen

Made in the USA
Middletown, DE
24 April 2019